SURRENDER

To: Shira,
Live well!

Jill Collins

Publishing History

May 2015

Published by JC AXIOM

This book is based on fiction. Characters, names, occurrences, places and incidents are not real and are the product of the author's imagination or are used fictitiously. Any resemblance to actual persons, living or dead, events, or locales is entirely coincidental.

THE HOLY BIBLE, NEW INTERNATIONAL VERSION®, NIV® Copyright © 1973, 1978, 1984, 2011 by Biblica, Inc.™ Used by permission. All rights reserved worldwide.

ISBN 978-0-9964515-2-9

Manufactured in the United States of America

DEDICATION

To Ural, Sadie, Lydia, Kim and God...

ACKNOWLEDGMENTS

To the family and friends who believed in me,
supported, listened, and loved me through this book,
you know who you are. I will forever be grateful.
Thank you Ural and Sadie Hutchinson for being my
mother and father and for blessing me with my siblings
Duque, Eric, and my consummate friend and sounding
board, Lydia. I would also like to give special thanks to
my husband, Kim, for being an inspiration and my rock.
And finally, thank you God, for your grace and for
being in my life. I am nothing without you.

❧ CHAPTER 1 ❧

"I'm looking for Commander Slade!" I yelled through the window of my car to the police officer while flashing him my Special Investigations badge. He peered in and squinted his eyes as I adjusted my skirt. He suddenly tensed his posture as he zeroed in on my badge. He then began to wave excitedly toward the guard to open the big wrought-iron gate.

"Dr. Winters, drive through," the officer told me. "Commandah Slade's been expectin' ya."

As I slowly drove through the *fleur-de-lis*-encrusted gate, as I took in the calm of the secluded neighborhood. Both sides of the street were elegantly lined with moss-filled oak trees. *Yes, indeed,* I thought. For the first time ever, I had been allowed into one of the most exclusive gated communities in New Orleans—Audubon Place. Structure after structure of lavish two- and three-storied Queen Anne and Colonial-styled homes embodied the drive.

"That's it!" I remarked out loud, interrupting my own thoughts and refocusing on the house in question: 77 Magnolia Place, the Dean Estate. Except for the police cars stationed in front, the estate looked like an old plantation—majestic, white, and full of columns. I parked my car a few houses down and turned the engine off to observe the area. I closed my eyes for a moment and heard the desolate sounds of crickets chirping and leaves rustling from the steady autumn breeze.

"Ahhh," I sighed. "God's southern country. Beautiful."

My idyllic reverie was cut short by the sight of detectives congregating on the big porch. *That looks like Slade's team over there,* I thought as I got out of my car and headed over.

"Hey, guys," I addressed them. "How's it going?"

"Hey, Doc," said one of them. "It's going. We got another one."

"Yeah, unfortunately. Slade in there?" The group of detectives included Leblanc, Glapion, and Anders. They were members of Commander Slade's investigative team.

"Yep," said Leblanc. "Just go on in. You'll see him."

Reaching for a pair of crime-scene gloves and booties from the box sitting just outside the front door, I walked into the big old house, hearing only the muffled echo of my footsteps on the hardwood floors.

As I continued to move slowly through the manse, a grand piano basking in the glow of dusk-filled sunrays captured my attention. I peered into the area as much as I could without compromising the fragile yellow crime-scene tape. Behind the piano was a floor-to-ceiling bookcase with a shiny golden *objet-d'art* in the form of an old horn-speakered Gramophone displayed prominently on one of its shelves.

I leaned in closer. "Is that what I think it is?" I asked in a whisper. "I'll be. It is. That's a Grammy." I looked to my left, then to my right, for any signs of immediate life. None were in sight. *The coast is clear*, I thought as I lifted the tape and stepped into the room. Venturing closer to the trophy, I put my black-rimmed eyeglasses on and began to read its inscription: NATIONAL ACADEMY OF RECORDING OF ARTS AND SCIENCES, ALLISTER DEAN, JAZZ, BEST IMPROVISED JAZZ SOLO—1994, CRAISINS.

 I thought. *Humph—our dearly departed Mr. Dean is a Grammy winner.* I continued to scan the room, when a familiar voice echoed through the space: "That you, Wintahs?" I hastily made my way back to the other side of the tape.

"Slade?" I yelled back.

"Yeah, I'm in here!"

"Where?"

"In the kitchen!" I followed the lingering reverb of his voice.

There he was—Jackson Slade, Commander of Specialized Investigations for the New Orleans Police Department, standing at the end of a long black granite island in the middle of the kitchen. He was adjusting the knobs on a noisy, static-filled police radio—pretty much the same thing he was doing the last time I saw him.

"Slade," I said as we came face to face. Our eyes met with the excitement and ease of two friends.

"Lookin' good, Wintahs. Where ya at?" he said with his trademark New Orleans/Brooklyn accent while giving me the once-over, up and down. He then turned his attention back to his dysfunctional hand-held radio.

"You don't look so bad yourself, Slade," I replied as he looked back at me with his playfully crooked smile.

"Ya know, Wintahs, these things are crap. When ya want 'em ta talk to ya, ya can't get a peep out of 'em. And when ya want some quiet from 'em, ya can't shut 'em up. What's the deal, Doc?"

Slade's six-foot-two frame presented an odd mixture of Cro-Magnon masculinity, a warm smile, piercing light-brown eyes, a full head of thick, dark brown hair, and a receding waistline.

"You losing weight, Slade?" I asked my buddy.

"Yep, I was gettin' so big I was startin' ta bleed gravy ovah heah. Had ta do somethin'."

"What'd you do?" I asked him as we began to walk out of the kitchen.

"Strange thing I learned, Wintahs."

"Uh-huh," I suspiciously replied.

"Here it is. In ordah ta lose weight, I learned that ya can't have a bacon san'wich for breakfast, a hot sausage po'boy for lunch, and a seafood plattah for dinnah. I know. I know. Shockin' right, but true. Jus' findin' this out. Jus' findin' it out."

"Really?" I playfully asked.

"Yep. True stuff, Wintahs. Ready ta go see what's upstairs?"

"Let's do it!" I replied enthusiastically as we stood at the bottom of a grand, winding chestnut stairwell.

"What do you know so far?" I asked Slade as we began to go up the big flight.

"One body, shot three times, stabbed thirteen times. Pretty much jus' like the other two. But this one seems a li'l different."

"In what way, and who found him?"

"Seems like this one was staged. And as far as we know, the other ones weren't. A neighbor called the police because the dog wouldn't stop barking."

"But how was it staged?"

"Somebody took the time ta lay his body down outside the area we presume he was killed in, which is the bathtub. His arms were folded, and he was covered up ta his neck with the bedspread."

"Yeah, sounds personal. Anybody talk to the family, wife, kids yet?"

"We're workin' on it. Afta you." Slade held his left hand out, gesturing for me to take the lead as we reached the top of the stairs.

We proceeded through the long hallway and into what appeared to be the master bedroom. I began to experience some of the intense dis-ease I usually feel around murdered corpses. My hands grew cold. My heart began to race. My senses were heightened. So I tuned out the noise of the scene and surveyed the area: a king-sized bed in the middle of a spacious, soft lavender room, resting on a round elevated platform...a marble fireplace to the right, under a mantel filled with pictures of what appeared to be a happy couple on a ski slope...but no signs of a crime, let alone a murder, though it sure felt like it.

"I'm assuming the body is back there?" I inquired, gazing toward what appeared to be the master bathroom at the opposite end of the vast space we were traversing.

"Yep," Slade replied. I could hear the *snap, click, click, snap, snap* of camera flashes and shutters from that direction—clearly the sounds of investigators taking pictures of a crime scene.

Young Detective Anders from Slade's team popped out from there, clutching an iPhone in a plastic bag. "Got the phone, Commander," he told Slade. "Haven't been able to crack the code yet, though."

Slade shook his head in dismay. Anders turned toward me. "Hi, Dr. Winters."

"Can I see it?" I asked him.

"Sure," he replied, handing the bagged phone to me. I held it in the air and scrutinized it carefully. I then pressed the round button at the bottom and swiped the 'Slide to Unlock' prompt. 'Enter Passcode' flashed on the screen. I punched in the numbers 1, 9, 9, 4. "We're in," I said.

"What?" Anders reacted in wide-eyed surprise.

"We're in," I confidently reiterated as I smiled and handed the phone back to him.

"How'd you—what'd you type in?"

"One-nine-nine-four."

"One-nine-nine-four?"

"Yeah, Nineteen-ninety-four. It's the year engraved on that Grammy sitting in the bookcase downstairs."

"Grammy?"

"You heard the lady, Anduhs," Slade interjected. "We're in. Now staht goin' through the phone."

We approached the master bathroom as Anders navigated the phone. I was hyper-focused on the only thing I could see in there: the feet of the victim. Investigators were blocking the rest of his body from my sight. Suddenly, a loud, familiar, shrill of a voice began to make itself known, startling me away from my preoccupation.

"What are you *doing? Look at me!*"

"But Dr. Haddock, the chief said to—"

"I don't *care* who told you to do *what!* I am the lead medical investigator here. The coroner. And I said to take the pictures first, *then* talk to the officers. And guess who I am? Come on. You know the answer."

Dr. William Haddock filled the air with a condescending laugh as he looked down at his young assistant investigator, who just stood there, eyes wide with fear, as he went on to answer his own question. "I'm your boss. So all actions, considerations, questions, answers, decisions, concerns, thoughts, queries, hunches *go through me! Got it?* You take the pictures, establish and *document* a chain of custody. *Then,* and only *then*, do you evaluate the scene. *Got it?*" Haddock squawked as the flustered, meek investigator transfixed on him in inescapable embarrassment. I watched her jaw tighten as she swallowed deeply, and her complexion turned cherry-red. In consolation to the young investigator, no one seemed to pay attention to the spectacle. We had all seen it before.

But I had heard more than enough. And I could tell Haddock was just getting warmed up.

"Slade, don't you have a filled-out chain-of-custody sheet?" I asked.

"Yeah."

"Give it to me."

"Huh?"

"I'll explain later. Just give me your copy."

"Whateva, Wintahs. Here." Slade handed me his copy of the document as I proceeded to insert myself into Haddock and his investigator's contentious colloquy. I glanced at her ID badge.

"Foy, right?" I asked her. She shot me a fearfully guarded expression. Not waiting for her answer, I went on: "Well, I want to thank you for being so helpful to everyone here. This is yours, right? Thank you very much." I handed her the chain-of-custody document.

"Ahhh, yeah? You're welcome," Foy timidly replied, still not knowing whether or not to trust anything that was going on.

"You had one done already?" Haddock asked the tormented assistant. "Why didn't you tell me?" He threw his hands up in disgust and walked away.

I edged away from Foy and said to Slade, "Boy, did that feel good. I just get tired of him being such a bully."

"I don't think Chief Deputy Coroner Haddock appreciated that," Slade said jokingly. "I think I saw one of the three hairs combed over the top of his head stand up. And here he comes again!" We laughed as we saw Haddock approach us, sneering.

"Well, well, well, if it isn't Dr. Morgan Winters sticking her nose where it doesn't belong—oh, that's right, you're here to 'help out,' " Haddock quipped contemptuously while making air-quote gestures with his fingers and peering at me over the top of his thin, black-rimmed glasses.

"So annoying," I muttered under my breath. Slade looked at me and rolled his eyes.

"All right, Haddock you know why I'm here, so spare all of us the drama," I calmly told him as I began to walk around the body while turning down the noise of Haddock and the other investigators and turning up the volume of the crime-scene visual.

A white male lay in the middle of a rather large, sleek brownstone bathroom on a black sheepskin rug in front of a Jacuzzi tub. I gazed at his lifeless face. He looked almost peaceful. His body was anything but peaceful, though: one, two, three, four, five, six, seven, eight, nine, ten, eleven, twelve, thirteen stab-wounds I counted, barely able to distinguish knife from bullet punctures. His hands were carefully placed over his midsection. His legs were clearly pulled together.

He didn't die like that, was my last thought as I began to lower the volume of my musings and increase that of everyone and everything else around me. The clicks and snaps of cameras, the static chatter of police radios, and the whispery prattle of conversation eased back into audio focus. I slowly made my way back over to Slade and Haddock's powwow.

"Aww, yeah, this one's just like the other ones," Haddock was telling Slade. "White male, stab wounds and gunshot wounds."

"This one seems to be a little different though," I chimed in.

"What are you talking about?" Haddock piped up. "And who asked you, anyway? Man shot several times, stabbed even more times. I know you got those crime-solving smarts and all, and I'm just the coroner around here, but I can guarantee you, I know what I'm doing."

I took his contemptuous retort as my cue to exit. I stayed in earshot long enough to see if he would reveal anything other than confirmation of his personality disorder. He didn't—but Slade's radio did.

"What's that? Repeat that," Slade spoke urgently into his radio. "Another body found in the park? Okay, we'll get over there some time tonight."

"Did I hear that right?" I asked him.

"Yep. Got another one in the park. That makes three in the park now, and this one. We got ourselves a mess on our hands."

"Commander. I think you need to see this," Detective Anders insisted as he approached Slade and myself.

"What is it?" Slade replied.

"We got at least twenty text messages from an unknown number, stating that he'll meet the victim at the gym or that he or she is at the gym. All of um are signed off with hearts and kisses emoticons." Anders said as he handed Slade the phone. I leaned over looking at the messages.

"Yep, 'I'm at the gym Alli, with a heart' is the last text on the phone," I chimed in as Slade and I then looked at each other pondering the text.

◈ CHAPTER 2 ◈

"Stop," I said in a breath-filled sigh as he slid his hand up my skirt. "Oh, God," I whispered in stifled ecstasy. "We can't do this."

But he wouldn't stop. He knew I didn't mean it. I attempted to pull away from his broad shoulders. But with one of his massive hands grasping the small of my back he jerked my body so close to his that I felt every inch of his desire for me. He was tall, lean, and muscularly framed.

In a deep, seductive voice, he whispered into my ear, "Stop pretending like you don't want me."

"No, I don't," I whispered.

"You're lying," he demanded, pulling me even closer. The intense heat of his body against mine, the smell of his cologne, overpowered me. I wanted him so badly that my will to fight was all but gone. "This is mine, and don't you forget it," he insisted...

*　　*　　*　　*

At 5:30 a.m. Monday morning, my alarm clock jolted me awake to the tune of "Wake Up, Everybody" by Harold Melvin and the Blue Notes. Lying face down, my long dark brown arms stretched from one end of the bed to the other. I dreaded the thought of peeling myself off the sheets. "You wake up," I mumbled in reply to the song rocking on the radio as I hit the snooze button. Drifting back into that faintly satisfying snooze-sleep...I could feel the pressure of four paws pouncing on my back.

"Maslow!" I yelled, lifting my head from under the pillow. There he was, his nose inches away from mine, my Jack Russell Terrier, Maslow. He snuck in a wet kiss and was gone.

"Okay, I'm up. I'm up," I begrudgingly grumped as I yanked the covers back and sat up on the side of the bed. Schlepping my bare feet onto the cool hardwood floors and into the bathroom, I gazed into the mirror, rubbed my almond-shaped eyes, turned the faucet on, and splashed cold water onto my face. I gave the mirror one more hard stare as I silently chastised myself for my lapse in judgment. I disapprovingly lifted an eyebrow, twisted my mouth to the side, and shook my head.

"Not good, Morgan!" I said out loud as I began to take off the white tank I had worn to bed. I snatched my sports bra and black jogging tights hanging on the back of the bathroom door and slipped them on. I laced up my Nikes, grabbed my keys and phone, opened the front door, inhaled a gulp of good ol' New Orleans liquid air, and began my morning run.

*   *   *   *

"Good morning, Kendall. How are you doing?" I asked my petite Cajun receptionist Kendall Roy as I pertly strode through the front door of my office at 8:50 a.m.

"Oh, I'm jus' fine Doc," she replied. How *you* doin'? Here, take a whiff of this." She handed me a cup of her famous dark roast chicory coffee.

"I'm good, Kendall." I took a sip. "Really good now."

"That reminds me, Doc. Didn't you tell me you had a date this weekend?" Kendall impishly grinned as she took a sip of coffee.

"Well, Kendall," I began, twisting my mouth to the side.

"Oh, no, Doc! Not another one!

"Yeah, another one—it didn't go well at all," I replied, omitting the second date I'd had later that evening.

"Awww. Lawd, Doc. That bad?"

"When he wasn't staring at my chest, he was talking about his mother or his ex-wife. Need I say more?"

"No, no, that's enough," Kendall affectionately said, shaking her head from side to side.

"Who's up first?" I asked her.

"That's her right there," she whispered as a statuesque, medium-brown-complexioned woman strutted through the outer doors. She stood about six feet. She wore a white-silk blouse, body-hugging gray slacks, and red stilettos. I discreetly smiled at Kendall—an enviable acknowledgment of the newcomer's good looks. Kendall rolled her eyes, raised her eyebrows, and nodded to me in agreement as she handed me a folder. Then she turned to the new client.

"Ms. Carlisle?" Kendall asked her.

"Yes," she responded in a watered down British accent. "I'm here to see Dr. Winters."

"Yes, ma'am. If you'd jus' have a seat over there, Dr. Winters will be right with ya, dawlin'. Okay?"

"Thank you," Ms. Carlisle quietly replied as she picked up a magazine and took a seat.

I opened the folder and scanned its contents. *Hmmm*, I thought, *Ivy Carlisle, model (super model). I thought she looked familiar. That would explain her striking good looks. No medications, no disease, mother was a stripper, father an alcoholic, can't maintain an intimate relationship, bursts of uncontrolled anger, feeling depressed and alone.*

I closed the folder and extended my hand to greet the super model. "Hi, Ms. Carlisle," I said, shaking her hand. "I'm Dr. Winters. Right this way." I held the door open as Ms. Carlisle gracefully walked past me. We went into my office. "Have a seat," I said. She sat on the edge of the brown sofa across from my chair. Her long legs were crossed and slanted to the side. She maintained very little eye contact. She was guarded. I waited a moment for her to look up. When she did, I smiled. She smiled back.

"Do you mind if I take my shoes off?" I asked. "My feet are killing me." She squinted her eyes and subtly smiled in curiosity.

"No, I don't mind," she said.

"Oh, great. I always like to ask. I promise you my feet are good. They just hurt." I removed my four-inch gray pumps, put them aside, and focused my full attention on Ms. Carlisle.

"Okay," I began, "let's talk about you, Ms. Carlisle, and why you're here."

Her smile quickly diminished as she looked down. "I'm here because I *have* to be here," she mumbled. Noticing her discomfort, I decided to digress from the subject of what brought Ms. Carlisle to my office. *I'll get back to that later.*

"So, I see it says here that you're a model. I thought you looked familiar. Tell me about that. What's it like to be a model?"

Her pronounced red lips grew into a comfortable smile. "Well, Dr. Winters," she said. "It's hard work, but I love it. Time evaporates when I'm in front of the camera or on the runway. It's my calling. I remember one time the paparazzi followed me for miles and…"

For twenty minutes, Ms. Carlisle vivaciously related stories about modeling, fans, and the business. Clearly we had established a connection. With that, I began to ask her more probing questions.

"Boy, those are some great stories," I interjected. "I feel like I have a good idea of who Ivy Carlisle, the fashion model is. But now I'd like you to tell me about Ivy Carlisle the woman, and what brought you here."

Ms. Carlisle's face grew serious and annoyed. "What's there to tell?" she asked with a tone of protest. "You know what happened? I'm a celebrity, and things happen. People are always accusing me of things. I'm under constant scrutiny, and I was defending myself. I don't know why they made such a big deal outta this anyway. I didn't do anything."

Her sudden lack of eye contact and her constant nose-rubbing had blaming dishonesty written all over it. "Ms. Carlisle," I said sternly, "this report says that you hit one of the other models and took a swing at your photographer. Then you smashed his camera equipment."

Back came her eye contact, along with a hint of the temper that had brought her into my office in the first place. "I compensated him!" she angrily replied. "What do you want me to say, Doctor? You wanna ask me about what happened? Do it. But I was only protecting myself. Okay? Actually, I've put it behind me. I'm trying to move forward."

I paused for a moment. I uncrossed my legs and leaned forward toward my guest, looking away only to put down my ink pen and pad. "Listen, Ms. Carlisle," I told her straightforwardly. "You're absolutely right. We want to deal with the here and now." I noticed her increased anger. "But, in order for me to help you and sign that release form, we're going to have to talk about everything, including the stuff you don't want to talk about—in fact, specifically what you *don't* want to talk about. You're not here for me. You're here for *you*."

She looked down and then up, as if searching for what to say. "I don't want to do this," she said meekly. "I don't want to be here. This doesn't feel good."

"Thank you for your honesty," I responded. "That's what we're going to be doing in here—being honest. Can I tell you what I'm thinking?"

She nodded her head and shrugged her shoulders in resignation.

"I'm thinking that I so understand not wanting to feel bad or talk about things that make you feel bad," I continued. "But hear this." I leaned closer toward her. "People who are hurting either feel the pain and deal with the hurt, or they attempt to ignore the pain and hurt themselves or others. I know, behind all that beauty, fame and money, you, are hurting. There are no shortcuts here."

I looked at the clock. Our time was up. "Same time next week, Ivy?"

She nodded in the affirmative.

The intercom buzzed as I closed the door behind Ms. Carlisle, quickening my thoughts back to the here and now. I answered the intercom. "Yeah, Kendall?"

"Doc, I have Commandah Slade on line one."

"Thanks. Send him through."

"You're welcome, Doc."

"Slade, hey, what's going on?" I asked as he came on the intercom.

"Can ya meet me at the Cathedral at noon?"

"Sure. Something going on?"

"Just meet me at noon. Okay?"

"Okay."

✥ CHAPTER 3 ✥

Sacred Heart Cathedral was an impressive century-old wood, stone and marble structure with stained-glass windows. Every now and then, Slade and I would meet there when we wanted to talk about a case in private. It was easy for me to embrace the automatic sense of security and comfort in a church. I opened one of its massive double doors and walked in.

Monsignor Paul Keegan, the pastor, was at the front of the church, lighting candles. He gave me a slight wave and a proper nod as he saw me enter. "It's been a while since I've seen you, Doctor," he said stoically while continuing to light candles. "What brings you to Sacred Heart in the middle of the day? Would I be correct in assuming that you're here to meet Commander Slade?"

Conversations with Msgr. Keegan were usually cordial and brief. Oddly, his favorite thing to talk about other than Scripture was his extensive gun collection. As I began to reply to his question, the sound of one of the church doors being shut made itself known. Both the Monsignor and I looked toward the entrance to see Slade walking in.

"Where ya' at, Wintahs? Hey there, Monsignor." He said greeting both of us.

"Why hello, Commander Slade," Msgr. Keegan responded cordially. "How are you?"

"One of those days, Monsignor—one of those days," Slade replied with a grimace as he stopped midway up the church isle to genuflect.

"So sorry to hear that, Commander. I'll say a novena for you during my afternoon prayers."

"'Preciate that, Monsignor. 'Preciate it."

Msgr. Keegan slowly blinked his eyes and nodded his head, acknowledging Slade's thanks. "Well, I'm going to be on my way now," he said. "You two probably want to talk, and I'm done here."

"Okay, Monsignor, see ya next time," Slade said.

"Bye-bye, Monsignor," I added as Msgr. Keegan proceeded behind the altar and into the sacristy.

Slade and I sat in the second row of pews. "What's going on?" I asked in a voice slightly louder than a whisper.

He turned toward me with a look of complete disquiet. "I think we got somethin' really bad goin' on here," he said forthrightly.

"Talk to me."

"I tell ya, Wintahs, between the two of us, I'm startin' ta believe... Wait a minute."

"Yeah, I feel it too," I whispered. "Feels like we're being watched."

Just then, *crash* went a loud noise from behind the altar. Slade reached for the gun that was sitting on his waist. I grabbed for the Taser in my purse.

"Everything okay back theah?" Slade's question echoed through the sanctuary but was met with silence. "Everything okay back theah? Monsignor?" Slade repeated in a louder tone.

Exaggerated quiet continued to linger in the air, until a lone voice broke the hush. "Ahh, no, it's me, Cameron," a fragile, slightly quivering male voice echoed. "Eh— everything's okay."

Out from behind the sacristy came a wiry, hunched-over, pale-complexioned man. It was the church custodian, Cameron Grimes. "Uhh, I dr...dropped something," he timidly said.

"It's okay, Mr. Grimes," Slade said reassuringly. "Just making sure you're okay."

"Oh, yes. Uhh, I'm okay, I guess. Just a li...little clumsy," Cameron slightly stuttered in reply in an air-filled wheeze of a laugh as he walked back behind the altar.

Slade and I looked at each other in curious relief. Then I gestured to him for us to take a walk and talk. He quickly refocused his attention back to the matter at hand. "We have four murder victims that for some reason are suddenly being pushed aside," he said. "The more I try ta do my job, the more the higher-ups scatter like cockroaches. I'm startin' ta realize I'm being given the run around. Things were movin' along fine when we discovahed the first two. Now, all of a sudden, life is hard. Can't get a subpoena to save my life. So, from now on, you're gonna know what I know."

"What about Bryson?" I asked.

"What about him? He's started draggin' his feet just like the rest of um, which ain't like him. He usually likes things done right. I don't know if it's about the bad press or what, but somethin' stinks, and I'm one o' the few not in on it. So do your thing, Wintahs."

"You got it," I replied as I reached for the stack of files, he was handing me, attempting to contain my excitement.

✥ CHAPTER 4 ✥

"Aww, man, four-thirty," I moaned as I looked at the clock. The guilt-ridden flashbacks of the feel of Cole's thick red lips kissing my neck had invaded my sleep again. I shook my head trying to clear my mind...only to have those thoughts replaced by the palpable reality of a serial killer in our midst.

I was wide-awake now. So I did what I usually do when I can't sleep: go teleshopping and read crime-scene reports—yeah, I know, not the best way to cope with discomfort. But, truth be told, most of us reflexively look for an easy button to help us escape the bad or painful things we feel. My practice is full of people spending their lives denying, suppressing, running from, or ignoring in order to maintain a delusional status quo, only to be let down by reality. It's a fool's paradise. And right now, I'm going for it.

*   *   *   *

"What's that? Yes it is," I excitedly whispered while sitting in the middle of my bed, remote control in one hand, phone in the other. "Isaac Mizrahi's cross-bodied leather bag—mine," I said as I dialed into my late-night companion, QVC, to make a purchase. The gratification was immediate. I then put the phone and remote control down to move on to my next indulgence. I began thumbing through the police reports Slade had given me:

Victim: Ronan Tate, White male DOB-6/20/82 (31 yrs), approx. 6'-0" (180 lbs.), found lying face down. Appeared to be blunt force wounds to right side of head, large bruise on left side of face, possibly due to fall, bruised wrists and ankles, due to duct tape, a considerable amount of blood under head and midsection. Gunshot wound to the back of the head. Abdominal stab wounds.

Victim: Paige Brook, White female DOB-8/2/84 (29 yrs), approx. 5'-4" (128 lbs.), found lying face down. Appeared to be blunt force wounds to right side of head, large bruise on left side of face, possibly due to fall, bruised wrists and ankles, due to duct tape. Considerable amount of blood under head and midsection. Gunshot wounds to the back of the head. Abdominal stab wounds.

Victim: Victoria Gaines, White Female DOB-12/15/80 (33yrs), approx. 5'-9" (140 lbs.), found lying face down. Appeared to be blunt force wounds to right side of head, large bruise on left side of face, possibly due to fall, bruised wrists due to duct tape, a considerable amount of blood under head and midsection. Gunshot wound to the back of the head. Abdominal stab wound.

Victim: *Allister Dean, White Male, DOB-7/2/78 33 year old, approx. 6'-2" 190 lbs., brown hair, muscular build, found lying with face down, blunt force wounds to right side of head, wounds to the back of his head. Victim appears to have been shot three times in the back of the head. Three abdominal stab wounds. Heavy blood stains beneath head and midsection. Body moved and covered with bedding.*

I flipped through a few more pages. *Dean's different, but they all died the same way,* I thought. *What are they doing? There's hardly anything here in the notes. Why are they stalling? Where's the preliminary autopsy report? We have a serial killer in uptown New Orleans, the Audubon Killer...*

I thought as I drifted off to sleep.

*   *   *   *

Later the next morning at my office, I found myself attempting to conjure up a profile of the person I was now calling "the Audubon Killer."

"Look at this, Kendall," I told her. "These reports show positioning of both bodies being pretty much the same—their hands at their sides, the number of wounds, how and where the wounds were inflicted are all the same—but Allister Dean's arms were *crossed over* his body, as opposed to being at his side, and he was moved. I feel like these reports are missing some information. They usually have more data than this."

"Really?" said Kendall.

"Yeah, strange, but I'm going to work with what I've been given."

"That's right Doc. Now, Mr. Dean is the one that you saw last week in Audubon Place, right?"

"Yeah. Not exactly sure why a 'little' more care was taken with him. One was found in his home. The other ones were found in Audubon Park bathrooms by people wanting to use the toilet. Almost everything else is the same, though. Kind of hard to profile this one. But I'm gonna give it my best try."

"Yeah, that's right, Doc. Give it a try." Kendall replied, waiting for me to go on.

"Let's see. He, the killer, might have a little age on him, maybe in his early 40s. The fact that all the victims are white lends to the probability that the killer is white too. He probably looks like your average Joe, to blend in—seeing as we don't have any witnesses who saw anything out of the ordinary in the neighborhood. We also know that most serial-killers take something from their victims, right?

"Ya think he's a serial killer, Doc?"

"Don't know yet. But let's say he is. Serial killers often take something from their victims as some sort of a keepsake. The first thing I would look for would be something simple, like tanned lines on ring-fingers or wrists. But these reports don't show any pictures of the victims' hands, which is a bit strange. I know the pictures were taken, and all of the victims were married."

"Oh, I know you, Doc," Kendal said as she threw her hands in the air, closed her eyes, and tilted her head to the side as if she were shouting for joy, praising the Lord in church. "You gonna figure it out just like ya always do. And befo' you know it, sweet Jesus, *bam!* Somebody's gonna be goin' ta jail!"

I couldn't help but smile and receive my receptionist's heartfelt support.

"I'm jus' tellin' the truth, Doc. I'm jus tellin' it like it t—i—is," she said, smiling and nodding at me in the affirmative.

Kendall and I then turned toward the office front door as we saw and heard someone enter. It was Ms. Carlisle, back for her second visit.

"Oh, would you look at that," Kendall said. "She's here a li'l early, Doc. Here's her file."

"Thank you, Kendall. Give me about five minutes. Then send her in."

"Okay, Doc."

*　*　*　*

"How've you been since our last visit, Ivy?" I asked the statuesque model, who seemed a little more relaxed this time. "Tell me what's been going on."

"Well I've been doing some thinking."

"Okay. Thinking about what?" I nodded my head in curious affirmation as I took my shoes off.

"Well, about what you said the last time I was here."

"Which part?"

"Well, you said I needed to be honest, and that maybe I had something to do with what happened at the studio. Here's the honest truth, Doctor. I hit Delia, took a swing at the photographer, and trashed his equipment because I was angry. There, I said it. Whew, I feel so much better. That's it, Dr. Winters, right? That's what you wanted me to do, right?"

"Absolutely, Ivy. We're on the right track."

"On the right track. What else do I need to do? I even called Delia and my photographer and apologized. I know I shouldn't have done those things. I admitted it. It's over, right?" Her thick dark-brown eyebrows turned up with childlike impatient exasperation.

"Not quite over," I said. "What you did was awesome, though. I know that took a lot of courage. Well done." Ivy smiled with proud confidence at me. "But I have a question for you," I continued. "What were you so angry about?"

"I was angry at Delia and my photographer for being so inept."

"I'm going to challenge you to look deeper at what you were *really* angry about. Your photographer and Delia were just easy outlets for something you've got going on inside."

"What? Doctor Winters, I'm sorry, but I don't know what you're talking about."

"Ivy—has there been anything or anybody in your life that's caused you deep pain or hurt?" Her acute reaction to my last question brought my attempt to probe deeper to a halt. She began to seethe with anger and defensiveness. She sat up straight and folded her arms.

"I told you what happened!" she said stubbornly.

"Ivy, something else is going on."

"I don't know." She dug her heels in deeper and tightened her jaw. "I was just angry."

"What were you really angry about?" I quietly asked her.

She glanced off into the distance with a scowl.

"What were you really angry about?" I repeated. No answer. "Ivy, look at me." She slowly fixed her eyes on mine. "What happened?"

Her icy stare slowly began to melt into tears. She hid her face in her hands and mumbled through her sobs, "He's gone. He's gone. I've got to get out of here!"

She grabbed her red oversized purse and dashed out of my office in a huff, rushing past Kendall. "Can I put you down for the same time next week, Ms. Carlisle?" my receptionist asked her.

"Yes, whatever. That's fine," exclaimed the young model in hurried agitation as she bolted through the front door.

❧ CHAPTER 5 ❧

"Repeat after me: 'Suppression.' "

"Suppression!" the audience said in compliance.

"Webster's defines 'suppression' as 'the conscious intentional exclusion from consciousness of a thought or feeling," I told them. "I'm gonna break that sentence down and take it to a personal level. And this is a true story. My aunt Jane, whom I was named after—some of you might know my middle name is Jane. Anyway, Aunt Jane died a long slow death from complications due to dementia when I was thirteen. I loved her dearly. Besides my mother and father, there was no one else I was closer to. My heart was broken. Anyone here ever had someone's death break your heart?"

I raised my hand and looked out into the audience to see many others with raised hands.

"For me, and because she had dementia, it was like watching someone you love die over and over and over again," I continued. The attendees nodded and listened closely. "It got to be so painful that I eventually chose..." I paused to make room for the emotion of that memory. "It got to be so painful that I eventually chose to stop thinking—or, more honestly, *feeling*—as it related to my Aunt Jane. I just stopped. And you know what, in those moments it felt good not to feel bad. So for a while, I'd gotten really good at ignoring the bad feelings. I didn't want to feel bad, so I didn't, I thought to myself. This is great!"

I flashed a cocky, self-assured smile as the audience laughed.

"I'd even got to wondering why hadn't anybody told me about this magical here-today-gone-tomorrow, on-off-switch way of handling pain," I continued. "But, wouldn't you know it, the reason why no one told me about the switch was because it wasn't real. You can turn it off, but some time tomorrow, or the next day or the next year, it'll be back with a vengeance. It'll show up disguised as a good time in the form of liquor, or lots of sex, or an extramarital affair, or gambling, or anger. You got me? I learned as a young adult that if you don't let the hurt, the tears, the pain out, it gets acted out."

"How'd *you* act out, Doc?" yelled someone from the back of the room, cutting through the silence.

"That's a great question from the back of the room," I said, smiling and pointing in the direction of the voice.

"I did something so seemingly innocuous that you really had to be paying attention to me as a child to know it. I'd begun to read books obsessively and bite my fingernails. Oh, and one more little thing. I stopped crying. I bit my nails until they bled, and I read at the exclusion of family, friends, and any kind of social life. I'd become miserably lonely and alone, avoiding my pain, unwittingly bringing on the hurt times ten. I eventually had to feel it in order to get rid of it. I couldn't read it away. I couldn't shove it away. I couldn't ignore it away by biting my nails. I had to go through it. For you out there, when something really awful happens, do *you* just decide not to feel it anymore? Do *you* just say I'm just not gonna go there?"

The audience nodded again in accord.

"I don't want to think about that," I said. "I don't want to. I...I...I..." I paused, eyeing the audience. "I'm not going to think about it. I'll just go to the mall instead and spend some money. I'm not going to be sad about that. I'll watch TV for the next six hours. That hurts too much, but this drink sure feels good. Or, better yet, I'm just fine. Come on, lucky number seven. This is the same angry teenager or adult that does drugs instead of being allowed to cry or talk about seeing his brother and three of his friends being shot to death. They're giving me the signal to wrap it up. So in closing, here's my charge to all of you out there in earshot." The patrons sighed in disappointment.

The room quieted down even more as I got closer to the microphone, lowered my voice, and asked my audience, "Ask yourselves, 'What hurts have I been stuffing, hiding from, or trying to ignore? What am I avoiding? What have I more often than not traded feeling for?' Remember these words, if you don't deal with it, it's going to deal with you. Your decision not to feel will drive you to overeat, drink, gossip, hoard, abuse—you name it. Folks I'm talking about putting down the internal and external shields that are keeping you from feeling things that hurt you. Surrender to the pain and win the battle. Not doing so is killing us, and it's even driving some of us to kill others. Thank you. Good night, and enjoy the rest of the evening folks."

The applause slowly grew to loud cheers of appreciation as I departed from the podium.

"Dr. Morgan Winters!" boomed the master of ceremonies as he took my place and led off thunderous plaudits for me, a guest speaker at the annual Friends of the Community Banquet, one of the royal gatherings of New Orleans' political elite, fittingly held in the Waldorf-Astoria Ballroom at the Roosevelt Hotel downtown. This was also one of the few times I got to hang out with my old college buddy, Dr. Carla Sanchez, chief medical officer for Southern Forensic Pathologists, a privately owned business that performs autopsies. She also sat on the board of directors for the Friends of the Community, which was how I got to speak.

"And now," continued the emcee, "I'd like to introduce the finest leader a city could ever have, the honorable *Mayor Cash Flint!"* The crowd erupted in another round of boisterous applause as the mayor of New Orleans made his way to the podium.

While this was going on, I could see Slade making his way to my table. He was wearing his dress blues. *He does wear that uniform well*, I thought. "Where ya at, Wintahs?" he asked me as he arrived at the table and casually lifted the white tablecloth to peek at my shoeless feet.

"You know me well," I discretely said with a grimace as I pulled the cloth down and out of his hand. "Now, take a seat." He sat beside me, grinning impishly, as he placed one of the table's white cloth napkins on his lap.

"What'd I miss?" he inquired.

"Not too much," I said humbly. "As you can see, the mayor's giving us a mini-state-of-the-city-according-to-Cash address."

"Yeah, what I also see is that the gang's all heah—Flint, Haddock, Monsignor Keegan," Slade whispered through the clacks and clatters of metalware against china.

"Oh, by the way, Slade," I said, "can I hitch a ride home with you? Had to put the car in the shop."

"Sure, Wintahs," he eagerly replied.

"In closing, I'd like to thank the Archdiocese for putting on such a spectacular affair," the mayor continued as the crowd applauded. "I'd also like to thank them for honoring the NOPD and all the other city officials for their efforts in community service. It's been my honor to serve this community as your mayor. It's been my duty to *protect* this community as your mayor. And I believe that we've done so in spades. The hard work of your New Orleans Police Department has been none other than exceptional. We put you first. We put you first. We put you first."

The applause grew into a standing ovation as the charismatically charming Mayor Flint ambled away from the podium, waving and smiling to his constituents. I turned to Slade, and we both shrugged our shoulders in wonderment of the effect this man had on people.

"Look at ya friend, Wintahs," Slade said humorously as we continued to applaud. "He's got 'em eatin' outta the palm of his hand. Doesn't even mattah what the crime numbahs ah. They love 'im." He turned to notice something. "Hey, isn't that ya friend Dr. Sanchez up theah, waving?"

I turned and was excited to see my old college chum again. "Yep, that's her," I replied, waving back to Carla as she stepped down from the panel seating.

"Hey, you!" Carla exclaimed as she made her way to our table.

I stood up to greet my friend. "Hey, woman. How are you?" We hugged.

"Muy bien, mi amiga," Carla said in her native tongue. *"Muy bien."*

"Carla, you remember Commander Slade, don't you?"

"Do I remember Commander Slade? Of course, I remember Commander Slade. Jackson, right? Good to see you again."

"How ya doin', Dr. Sanchez?" Slade extended his hand.

"Oh, I don't think so. I want a hug from you. And you better call me Carla." The curvaceously petite brunette extended both arms toward Slade, as they embraced.

"Well, sit down for a minute, Carla," I said. "Tell me, what's been going on? How are Frank and the kids and that job?"

"Heah, take my seat," Slade offered as he stood up. "I see some folks I need ta talk to. I'll be back in a few. Carla, always a pleashah." He sauntered away.

"I'm fine, Morgan," Carla told me. "Frank, the kids, and work are good. I'm just so busy. You know, when I took that chief medical officer job, I had no idea how much time it would require—wait a minute! Here I am, talking about how busy I am. What about you? I can't turn on the TV these days without hearing about some crime being solved by the brilliant Dr. Winters. How are you?"

"Well, I don't know about all of that, but the NOPD is keeping me busy."

"But Morgan, if I know you like I think I know you, you love it. Don't you?"

"You know I do. I get such a rush from peeling back the emotional layers of people that commit crimes. Don't get me started."

"Okay, okay, all that's great. But what's going on *outside* the job?"

I squinted my eyes and looked at Carla as if I didn't know what she was getting at.

"Don't look at me like that," she said. "You know exactly what I'm talking about. What about the love life? What's going on? Better yet, what's going on with that hunk Commander Slade is the real question. Y'all have been friends for a while now, and I think he likes you."

"You do? Well, there is absolutely nothing going on with Commander Slade. We're just friends."

My friend tilted her head and twisted her mouth to the side. She didn't believe me.

"Well, then, who *is* there something going on with? Really! Because I—" Carla interrupted herself and redirected my attention with her eyes to the tanned, six-foot-three, broad-shouldered superintendent of the New Orleans Police Department, Cole Bryson, approaching our table.

"Dr. Winters, how nice to see you again," Superintendent Bryson said in the deep, commanding voice that was his trademark.

"Good to see you too, Superintendent," I replied, politely smiling.

"Dr. Sanchez," the superintendent said to Carla.

"Superintendent." They shook hands. He then turned to me.

"Dr. Winters, I was wondering if I could meet with you tomorrow to discuss a new psychological exam we're considering. It shouldn't take up too much of your time. Would you be available tomorrow?"

"Ahh, tomorrow's a busy day for me," I said.

"Well, what about the day after that?"

"Ahh, I'll have to check my calendar. I'll get back with you."

"When might that be?"

"Let's say tomorrow," I quickly replied, not wanting the conversation to linger.

"I look forward to your call tomorrow, Doctor," he said eagerly. "The force appreciates everything you do. You have a good evening, now, okay?" He coyly glanced at me in a way that only I could see. He widened his eyes and slyly smiled at me, then glanced at Carla.

"Dr. Sanchez," he said cordially as he left the table.

"Superintendent," Carla replied as we both watched him walk away.

"He's a good-looking cocky something, ain't he? I just..." Carla once again interrupted herself in mid-thought, this time to see the mayor approach our table.

"Evenin', everybody," said the always-charming Mayor Cash Flint as he smiled glad-handedly at us. "Y'all enjoyin' the festivities? I *thought* that was you sittin' over here, Morgan. It's been a while. How ya doin'?"

"I'm doing well, Mr. Mayor," I said, a bit formally.

"Oh, now you stop that, Morgan. We've known each other far too long for all that. I'm still jus plain ol' Cash."

"Well, plain ol' Cash, I don't need to tell you how well-received your speech was. They love you."

"Aww, thank ya, dawlin'. Ya know I'm just out here doin' what I can for the community," he loudly articulated as he smiled and peered around the table, knowing all eyes were on him. "Dr. Sanchez, right?" he suddenly said as he looked at Carla and extended his hand.

"That's right, Mr. Mayor," she said as she shook his hand. "So good to see you again."

"Same here, Doctor. You've really made a difference sitting on the board of directors for this event. It gets better each year. Good to have some diversity." He turned back to me. "Well, Morgan, I'm not gonna keep ya from all this good food here. I just wanted to stop by ta say hi to ya and tell ya I'd love to stop by your office ta see ya new digs."

"Any time, Cash, any time."

"And maybe we can have one of our old chats, huh?"

"Would love to." I felt uncomfortable, yet kept my composure.

"Well y'all enjoy the rest of the evenin', okay?" the mayor said as he walked away, smiling and waving goodbye to anybody he could.

"See what I mean, *mi amiga?*" Carla quipped to me humorously. "You're a big shot. They're not coming over here to see *me.*" We both chuckled.

"And I tell you another thing. I like Mr. Commander Slade, but if I didn't know better, I'd swear that something was going on with you and the Superintendent, the way he looked at you."

I playfully rolled my eyes. My old friend eyed me with familiar scrutiny. I couldn't fool her. Truth be told, I didn't want to. I was ready to unburden myself. "All right, you. Come with me," I told my friend as I put my shoes on and then grabbed her hand. We walked across the ballroom toward the grand white French doors leading to the terrace.

*   *   *   *

"It was some time ago on a Saturday night. I found myself feeling particularly sad and alone. I was missing Charles. He'd only been gone about six or eight months. Dammit! We'd only been married a year when God decided it was time for heaven to have him. Anyway, I'd just moved back here, and I was trying to hold it all together."

"Yeah, I remember how hard it was for you when Charles died so suddenly."

"Yeah. It was. So, that night, wanting to escape from myself, I decided to go to Loraine's Jazz Cafe. You remember Loraine's?"

"Yeah, I remember Loraine's. It's that little club in the Marigny on Frenchmen, right?"

"Yep. Well, that night, I brought my violin and sat in. Carla, I played every note with passion-filled perfection. It felt so much better to play my violin than to feel the hurt of missing Charles."

"I know, *mi amiga,* I know." Carla put her hand on mine as I took a sip from my glass of wine.

"Well, as the night went on, I found myself locking eyes with a stoically handsome man sitting at a table in the corner of the room. I looked away, but I could feel him watching my every move. He even led a standing ovation for my rendition of a Prince song."

"Which song?"

" 'Still Waiting.' Remember that one?

"Oh, yeah. It's full of sadness."

"Yes it is. By the end of that song, the tall, handsome man in the corner had made his way to the stage. He said, 'Hello, my name is Cole. And can I just say, I'm a fan. You play a brilliant violin. Can I have your autograph?' He winked his eye and gave me a sparkling smile. He then handed me a piece of paper and an ink pen. 'Oh, and if you could just write down your phone number, too, I promise this will be the beginning of a wonderful friendship.' His deep-set green eyes were penetrating. When I spoke, I could see him looking at my lips, as if there was no one else in the room.

"That night, Cole was just what the 'Doctor' ordered, in an unhealthy, not-dealing-with-my-pain kind of way. I was drowning my sorrows in his eyes and his devilishly handsome charm. I felt great! He'd mentioned he was a policeman. But I was new in town. So I didn't know who he was, and he wasn't the superintendent at that time. Honestly, Carla, that night I'd turned my receptors off anyway. I didn't want to know any truth outside of that moment.

" 'What, are you going to turn into a pumpkin? Or is it me? I thought you were enjoying my company,' he said with a sheepish grin as he stared into my eyes.

" 'No, it's not you,' I said. 'I have a very important nine a.m. appointment, and I'd like to be somewhat coherent for the meeting. So I need to get some rest and call it a night.'

" 'Of course you do,' he said as we walked to my car. In one sweeping motion, he gently slid his hand into mine, pulled me closer, and whispered into my ear, 'You're beautiful, Morgan Jane Winters.' Then he placed a soft of kiss on my right cheek. I briefly looked away, biting my lower lip and rolling my eyes in excitement. I did feel a tinge of discomfort from his subtle attempt to guilt-trip, or rather manipulate, me into staying longer, but I chose to ignore it. I didn't find out until later that he was married.

"But, Carla, I was running from myself. I just didn't want to miss Charles anymore, by any means necessary. So here we are. When I see him at events like today, you see what happens."

"Are you still seeing him? No judgment, *mi amiga*, just a question."

"No, I ended it a while back. But for a sad human flaw of a reason, I've periodically let him back into my life." I took another sip from my glass of wine. "That's the story. You're the first person I've shared this with."

"I'm just sorry you didn't tell me sooner. Anytime you need to talk, you call me."

"I know. Truth is that I need to deal with the grief of losing Charles. I still avoid it."

We were beginning to walk back into the noisy ballroom, when up came Slade. "There ya are," he said to me. "Been looking for ya."

"Call me," Carla said to me as we hugged each other. She walked back toward her seat.

"Ya ready ta get outta here?" Slade asked me.

I nodded in the affirmative.

"Let's roll," he said eagerly. We made our way to the exit and toward Slade's truck. Rain began to fall as we got in.

"Thanks for the ride, Slade," I said. "I owe you one. By the way, what's with not having any type of preliminary autopsy report?"

"You're preachin' to the choir, Wintahs. Nobody's budging. Also, just found out that we got Skylar Dean, Allister Dean's widow, comin' in. You want a crack at her?"

"What time?"

"Five-thirty."

"See you at five-thirty. I'm going to stop by the coroner's first, though, to see if I can get ahold of anything over there."

"Good luck on that," Slade remarked as it rained harder and an old song called 'Black Cow' by Steely Dan began to play on his car stereo. "Startin' ta come down now, huh?" he said, reaching for the volume and turning it up. We both sang along:

"Always wondahed what that song was about," Slade questioned as he lowered the volume slightly.

"It's about living a lie," I replied as I reached over and turned the volume back up. Slade momentarily took his eyes off the road, glancing my way, shrugging his shoulders. We continued to sing along.

❧ CHAPTER 6 ❧

Doing business in government buildings was becoming more and more of a hassle these days. We practically had to get MRIs done in order to get through the front door. But I understood why the extra security was necessary, so I did like most law-abiding citizens do: I fell in line and put my keys, phone and change into the plastic bowl provided. I placed my briefcase and purse onto the conveyor belt, and then stepped through the metal detector. Yippee, no extra beeps or noises as I walked through. I felt relief as I cleared the security hurdles.

"Good mornin', Dr. Winters," said an older red-haired security guard that had been watching me from the moment I walked in. His eyes were shadowed by long, unruly red eyebrows.

"Good morning," I replied as I removed my belongings from the end of the conveyor belt.

"Been a fan of yours since the Biegnet King case, Doctor."

"Is that so?"

"Yep. Oh, let me get that for ya." He reached for my briefcase. "I'm new at this buildin'. I was hopin' I'd run into ya one day, and today is that day. I think you're great, Dr. Wintahs. Can't tell ya how glad I am you moved back to New Orleans from New York to help the police. I'm your biggest fan. You workin' on those uptown murders, ain'tcha? They not talkin' 'bout much, but I know you workin' on 'em. Huh?"

"Thank you so much, Mr. Jones," I replied straightforwardly as I glanced at his ID badge. "I'm in a bit of a hurry. So I've got to get going."

"Oh, I'm sorry. Did I say somethin' wrong? I didn't mean ta."

"Not at all," I said as I noticed his change in continence. He raised his bottom lip and chin in what appeared to be embarrassment. He then turned up both sides of his mouth in childlike scorn. "It was wonderful to meet you," I said cordially. You have a great day, Mr. Jones."

"You, too," he mumbled as his demeanor somewhat softened and I made my way toward the elevator. *That was uncomfortable,* I thought. Ever since I had begun working with the NOPD, these types of encounters had been occurring more and more frequently. But that one seemed a bit more personal and unstable.

"Hi, Ms. Hill," I said as I glanced at the nametag of the young blond gatekeeper sitting at the front desk. "My name is..."

"I know who you are," she said brusquely as she vacuously looked up at me.

I ignored her flat, unwelcoming presence and went on to tell her why I was there. "I'm here to see Dr. Haddock."

"Hold on," she said in her same expressionless monotone while looking down at her appointment book. "Do you have an appointment?"

"No. So I would be very grateful if you could squeeze me in somehow."

She gave me another blank stare and began to write and mumble. Upon second glance, I realized that the stone-faced young lady I was talking to was the same person Haddock had publicly ridiculed at the crime scene in Audubon Place.

"Excuse me?" I politely asked.

She looked up at me and spoke in a slightly louder voice, "I said, I can't help it if people wisp by when I'm writing or when I'm at the copy machine." She then picked up several pieces of paper and left me where I stood.

Well, I surely didn't need a brick to fall on my head to get this one. I quickly made my way to Haddock's office. Knock, knock, knock.

"It's open," said a familiar, sarcastically demeaning voice on the other side of the door. I turned the knob and walked in to see him sitting behind his desk, writing. He knew someone was standing there, but he continued to write without uttering a word. This was his not-so-passive way of establishing some sort of one-upmanship, control, or whatever you want to call it over anyone who walked into his office. After a couple of seconds, I cleared my throat to get his attention.

"Be with you in a minute," he replied in a harsh, irritated voice as he continued doing what he was doing.

Enough of this, I thought. "William!" I piped up.

He immediately looked up in surprise. "Winters! What are you doing here?" He was clearly annoyed. "How'd you get back here?"

"I got nothing but answers for you, William. I came to see you, and I walked. Now I got a something for you. I need to see whatever you have on the uptown murders."

I observed irritation mixed with contempt in Haddock's face. He hated that I could ask him for information or a report, and that he had to give it to me.

"You want information? Fine. Sit here." He closed the folder on his desk and proceeded to leave his office. I did as he suggested. But then, I stood up and glanced at the name on the folder on his desk: Allister Dean. I stared at the folder as the temptation to open it began to take over. *There are no coincidences, Morgan. You are here right now for a reason. He's been gone almost five minutes now. But these people have a right to their privacy. But I'm trying to help them. I was torn.*

I slowly reached for the folder as I overheard Haddock barking at his gatekeeper, "I told you that absolutely nobody comes back here without being announced! I don't care what you have to do to make that a reality! Just do it!"

Haddock marched back into his office, startling my hand back into place. "Here," he said as he handed me a thinner folder. "Are we done?"

"Yes, we are. Thank you," I replied, getting up.

As I walked out of Haddock's office. I began to second-guess myself. *Did I miss an opportunity? Was there something there I was supposed to see? No, Morgan. Stop that. Things are happening just the way they're supposed to. Trust the process of life. This is more than I had when I walked in. I hope this meeting with Mr. Dean's widow offers something.*

*   *   *   *

"Good evening, Frank." I said to the front-desk officer as I entered the 15th precinct.

"Evening, Dr. Winters," Frank replied. "The Commander's waitin' on ya. Go on back."

I proceeded down the long hallway, hearing only the pronounced echo of my heels against the concrete floor. "*Hola mamacita*," catcalled a disheveled old man in handcuffs sitting in a holding area. As I walked past the area, I turned toward the old man and gave him a stern smile.

"What's your name? You sure look good," said another handcuffed man.

"*Mi amigo,*" said the first one. "You know who that is. It's that shrink catching all them murderers. That's Dr. Winters."

"Well, hey theah, Dr. Winters," a third man chimed in. "I got something for you to look at."

"Don't listen to 'em, Doc," said a scantily clad pretty young woman sitting in the same area, who was in handcuffs as well. "They haven't had their five o'clock feeding yet." I kept walking, but I did chuckle at her comment.

"Awww, Doc, ya leavin'?" yelled one of the cuffed men. "I was really lookin' forward to that exam!"

"Don't worry, you'll get it in the end, eventually," I retorted facetiously, unable to resist a reply. I then winked at the lone cuffed woman and kept walking.

"Oh, that's cold Doc," quipped another one of the men. "That one really hurt." The others laughed, howled and hooted.

"All right, all right. That's enough of that. Pipe down," Slade yelled as he appeared at the end of the corridor. I entered his office to see a very tastefully dressed, slender woman seated in one of the two chairs in front of his desk, her legs crossed and arms folded.

"Mrs. Dean, this is Dr. Morgan Winters with Special Investigations," Slade said to her, motioning toward me. "Dr. Winters, Mrs. Allister Dean."

"I know who you are," the lady cautiously said to me as she looked me over.

I extended my hand and gave her a warm smile, ignoring her protective veneer as we then shook hands. "Hello, Mrs. Dean. I'm so sorry for your loss. I'm here to ask you a few questions." Her apprehension was evident as she continued to watch my every move with intense eye contact and stoic expression. "This is going to be a little different than the other police interviews, Mrs. Dean," I continued. "I'd like you to relax as much as you can, and we're just going to talk. Okay?"

I took the seat next to her, and she compliantly nodded. Slade sat on a small, unassuming brown leather couch behind Mrs. Dean.

"Do you mind if I take my shoes off? My feet are killing me," I asked her, and she slowly nodded in the affirmative. I calmly removed my black pumps, took a deep breath, and exhaled. "I understand that you and your husband were married for quite some time," I began. "How long?"

"Ten years."

"That's a long time." She blankly waited for my next question. "Mrs. Dean, can I call you by your first name? It's Skylar, right?"

"Yes it is, and yes, you may," she politely responded.

"Ten years is something to be proud of. Tell me your fondest memory of your husband Allister." As I waited in silence for her reply, for the first time I saw a hint of emotion from her as her eyes began to glisten with tears. She swallowed, successfully fighting back the urge to cry. She then looked at me and began to speak.

"Allister was a warm, sensitive, gifted man, with the most intoxicatingly beautiful smile you could imagine. He'd sing and write music from the time he awakened. I told him my secrets. He told me his—I guess." She paused for a moment, staring off and away, then turned back toward me. "He was my best friend. We were planning a trip to the south of France. I loved him." She paused again and swallowed deeply. "It's hard to just talk about one moment. I loved him."

I could see the pain of loss in her eyes. It was so familiar. Her once erect, guarded posture had become soft—almost limp.

"Skylar," I ventured, "I don't know how you feel, but I know how I felt when my husband was suddenly taken away from me. It was hard to breathe. I kept playing our last conversation over and over again in my head. I still do it. It was my last memory. What was your last memory?"

Mrs. Dean suddenly tensed up again. She sat up straight and folded her arms in guarded protection. "What do you want to know, Doctor?" she asked.

I leaned forward, looked into her leery but pain-filled eyes, and softly asked her, "Did he smile? Did he hold your hand? Did he hug you? What was the last thing you saw in his eyes? What were the last words you remember hearing from him?"

She looked up toward the honest left, accessing her memory, as she then began to speak. "At about eight a.m. Thursday morning, my husband of ten years fixed our usual breakfast, eggs Benedict with ham and bacon. But that morning was different. He was full of nerves. I chalked it up to flight jitters. He knew I had a flight to catch, and he was trying to get me out on time. Now I know better. He even spilled a glass of orange juice.

"We sat there like we do most mornings, eating breakfast. But that day, he held my hand, told me how beautiful I was, and how much he would always love me. He then proceeded to ask me for a divorce. He said that he loved me but that he wasn't *in* love with me, and that he was in love with somebody else. He'd been having an affair."

Mrs. Dean vacuously looked at me and went on: "I didn't say a word to him. I got up and just left the house. I drove around for hours before I eventually went to the airport to catch my flight. That was my last conversation with Allister, Dr. Winters. That's what I remember."

I could see Slade's eyebrows rise as he sat behind her, listening. Clearly she had neglected to tell the police about that conversation. Slade sat up on the couch and impulsively asked her, "What time did you check in at the airport?"

Mrs. Dean stared off into the distance again. I slyly gave Slade the stink-eye for butting in. He raised his left eyebrow and rolled his eyes in apology while sitting back on the couch again.

"I don't know," she finally said. "I sat in the outer area of the airport before I checked in. My flight wasn't until three o'clock that afternoon. That was the last time I saw him alive."

By now her eyes were glassy with unwanted tears. She lost her battle for stoicism as a lone tear ran down her cheek. "I tried to forget about that morning, that day. I wanted to remember him, us, the way we were before all of this, before he told me that he wasn't in love with me anymore, before someone killed him. Haven't been able to though. I would imagine that hell would be more preferable than what I've been living in these days."

We sat in silence for a few moments. I reached for her hand. "Skylar, I can only imagine the pain you're in or how you must be feeling. I'm here to help find your husband's killer, but if I can help you, let me. I'm just a phone call away."

I put my card into her hand as she lifted her head, her eyes replete with tears. "Thank you," her quivering voice replied.

"Skylar, thank you so much for talking to me. I know this was hard, but it was very helpful."

"We'll contact ya if we need ta talk to ya again, Mrs. Dean," Slade said as he stood up. "We're gonna ask that ya don't leave town until further notice and that you surrender your passport. It'll just make it easier if we need any more information."

Mrs. Dean nodded, handed Slade her passport and walked toward the door. I followed her, watched her go down the hall for a bit, and then closed the door slowly and quietly and turned back to Slade.

"What the hell?" he remarked. "He was havin' an affaiah. Who knew? I tell ya, Wintahs, I don't know how ya do it. But she kept that ta herself until you. And I don' know what it would have taken for us to get that out of her."

"Slade, I think we saw a woman just starting to deal with her new reality," I volunteered. "She lost her husband twice—first to whomever he was having an affair with, and then to a murderer."

"Or, and then she killed him," Slade insinuated.

"Maybe, maybe" I replied.

"She had mo' than enough time to have left and come back and then leave again for the airport," Slade hypothesized. "And, yeah, I know at this point it would be pure speculation and circumstantial. But, boy, do we have a motive."

"Yeah, we have a motive," I said, "and I know you don't like it when I say this, but I don't get that vibe from her though."

"Aww, come on, Wintahs. You saw her. I learned this from you. She was emotionally detached for most of the interview. We don't know what she's capable of. We do know that she's capable of lying *by omission to the police.*"

"Yes, we do." I replied.

⁂ CHAPTER 7 ⁂

"Good morning, Doc. Ain't it just the most beautiful day outside?"

"It sure is, Kendall. How are you doing this morning?" I asked my receptionist, as if I didn't already know what her answer was going to be.

"Why I'm doin' jus' fine. Couldn't be better," she replied with that quarter-of-a-moon smile of hers as she handed me a cup of coffee. She then tilted her head to the side and looked up towards the right. Her imagination was at work. "What about those murdahs, Doc? I been tryin' ta put myself at those scenes and put some o' the pieces togethah. But I'm comin' up blank. Whatcha got new? I know you got somethin'."

"Funny you should ask, Kendall."

"I knew it. I bet it's juicy," Kendall said with a big grin. Her pupils had become slightly dilated—a sign she was excited.

"Well, you know, I spoke to Skylar Dean."

"Skylar Dean?"

"Yeah, you know. She's the wife of Allister Dean, the Audubon Place victim."

"Oh, yeah, yeah, that's right, that's right. I remember now. So, okay, you spoke to Mrs. Dean. *Skylar* Dean. Now, *that's* a name," Kendall said, as if she had just been given a very important piece to the puzzle. She sat on the edge of her seat, eagerly waiting for more.

"Yes, Skylar Dean. Slade and I met with her at the precinct. It seems as though Mrs. Dean was holding out on some very important information."

"What?"

"Her husband was having an affair."

"Go 'way from here!" Kendall retorted.

"Yeah, that was the first anybody had heard of this."

"You mean she lied to the police?"

"Only by omission. She just left that tidbit out. She told us that she found out about the affair the morning Mr. Dean was murdered."

"*Oooh, no!* Get the gun, Doc! Get the gun and shut the front door!"

"Yes, she did. And I tell you what—I don't know enough about her or their marriage to know the depths of her denial, but she also talked about how great their marriage was."

"Great like a jalapeno pepper, good goin' in, but butt-burnin' hot as hell comin' out!" She lowered her voice while nodding. "Right, Doc?"

I squinted my eyes in an attempt to visualize what I had just heard, but quickly changed my mind and continued: "She said they were best friends. In fact, they were planning a trip to the south of France, when, as she put it, her 'world came crashing down.' She said that prior to the conversation that morning. He was damn near perfect in her eyes."

"Well, you know what dear ol' Mother Franklin would say about that." Kendall paused and looked toward the heavens.

"What would Mother Franklin say about this one, Kendall?"

"Mother Franklin would say that, 'That happiness you feelin' is jus pain takin' a break.' 'Cuz can't nothin' be perfect. If you think it is, jus' look again. It ain't." Kendall nodded her head with the furrowed brow of convicted thought.

This time I'd have to say that Mother Franklin was probably right, I reasoned.

"But did she kill him, Doc? Did she kill him? Did she do it is what I wanna know, Doc. I tell ya, if Trevuh evuh stepped out on me, I'd be so mad I'm pretty certain I'd kill 'im dead and leave 'im for road-kill."

"Exactly! That's because you love your husband. I believed Mrs. Dean when she said that she loved her husband. This did not look like a crime of passion. So, no, I don't think she did it. Even though it was the same day that she not only found out her husband of ten years had been having an affair and that he was in love with this other woman."

"So ya think she was tellin' the truth—huh, Doc?"

"I think so. Even though I'd never met her before, and I don't know her daily body language, but I think I got a pretty honest read on her. When we talked, she consistently looked up towards the left, referencing memory, not her imagination. Her eye movement and eye contact were consistent with that of a person recollecting an event, as opposed to *creating* an event. She generally looked away and covered her eyes when she cried. Her posture was closed initially, which is normal. She didn't know me. She knew that she was in a police station being interviewed. The more she talked, the more relaxed and open her body language became. The most telling thing is that she told me about a hurt-filled, incriminating event that she'd left out of her interviews with the police."

"Well, you know, Doc, people tell you things they don't tell other folk."

"I agree. But in this case, I don't think she was trying to hide anything. I think she kept it from the police in order to maintain the delusion of the past. I don't think she wanted to face the new truth that had just been handed to her. Prior to that day, for her, life was great."

"Well, Doc, I do feel sorry for Miss Skylar, or for that matter anybody going through that kinda stuff. Oh, look. Your nine o'clock's here."

We looked toward the front door to see Ms. Carlisle walk in. "Ivy, good morning," I said.

"Good morning, Doctor. Good morning, Ms. Roy."

"Good mornin', Ms. Carlisle," Kendall echoed.

"You can have a seat in my office, Ivy," I said. "I'll be in in a moment." Kendall handed me Ms. Carlisle's folder. I surveyed my notes, refreshed my memory, and headed in.

"So, how are you Ivy?" I asked while removing my shoes and noticing that my court-ordered client appeared calmer this time. Her shoulders stood a little more relaxed, and her eye contact was more direct.

"I'm doing okay, Doctor."

"Tell me about your work week."

"Uhhh, I guess it's been okay." Ivy suddenly broke eye contact and looked away.

"Ivy, what happened?"

"Uhh, everything's okay now."

"What happened, Ivy?"

"Well, everything was fine until he started at me again."

"Who?"

"Miguel. He started criticizing me and telling me how to do my job again."

"What was he telling you?"

"How to stand, how to tilt my head. I know all that. I've been doing that for the last five years. I'm paying him." Her continence changed. Her eyes grew wide, and she began to seethe with irritation.

"What happened next?" I calmly asked her.

"I shoved him. He wouldn't knock it off. I told him to knock it off. If he would have just kept quiet, I wouldn't have had to."

"Can I interrupt you for a moment?"

"What?" she snapped in misdirected anger.

"I want you to breathe.

"What?"

"I said, *breathe.* Take a breath. Breathe in. Hold it. Now breathe out. Again. Breathe in. Hold it. Breathe out."

Ivy reluctantly followed my directions, inhaling and exhaling deeply. She sat back on the couch as her tension seemed to dissipate.

"That's better. Ivy, we've got a raging fire here that's causing you anxiety, court dates, money, your reputation, and threatening your freedom."

"Miguel?" Ivy asked.

"No, Miguel's not the cause. We'll deal with the cause of the fire in a minute, but right now, we need to put the fire out first—your temper."

"Oh."

"Do me a favor?" I asked.

"Okay."

"I want you to write this down: 'Another person's bad behavior has nothing to do with what I do. I am responsible for my own actions.' I want you to say this every time you feel like somebody has offended you, disrespected you, wronged you, looked at you cross-eyed. You get what I'm saying?"

I handed her a piece of paper and a pen. She hesitated, but eventually acquiesced to my request. "But he—" she began abruptly.

"He has nothing to do with what you do," I interjected. "You're powerless over him and what he says. But you do have power over yourself and how you respond. The reason why we're here today is because you've decided that someone else's behavior dictates what you do. It doesn't. That anger and what you're doing with it is coming from inside of you, not him or anybody else. Finish writing, Ivy. You can ask me anything, but write it down first. Do you need me to say it again? 'Another person's bad behavior has nothing to do with what I do. I am responsible for my own actions.'"

"I got it. I got it. But Doctor, I just get so angry."

"And that's okay. It's okay to get angry. Have your feelings. But you can't hit, demean, shove, push, or berate somebody because of how you're feeling. That's what some of us did when we were children. You're not a child anymore, Ivy. You're a beautiful, smart, outgoing young woman. And maybe it's time for the adult in you to take charge. That little girl and the woman before me are tired of all of the drama. Am I right?"

"You're right. I'm tired of this crap."

"So we're in agreement that another person's bad behavior has nothing to do with what you do?"

"We're in agreement."

"Good. There's a wise quote I know that declares, where two agree in statement of request, it shall be granted. So let's say this in agreement together, Ivy: 'Another person's behavior has nothing to do with what I say or do. I am responsible for my own actions.' Again."

As we chanted this phrase in unison, Ivy began to sit up a little straighter. "Good," I said. "Okay?" Ivy nodded in agreement. "Now," I continued, "let's try to deal with the reason for the fire. The last time you were here, you told me that somebody very important to you was gone. Who's gone, Ivy? Who were you talking about?"

Ivy sank back into the couch in what appeared to be unguarded despair as she put her head into her hand. After a few moments of silence, she said, "Ronan's gone," in a soft, fragile tone.

"Who's Ronan, Ivy?

"Ronan was the man I loved. He was murdered."

"Ronan Tate?"

"Yes, Ronan Tate. He was the best thing in my life. And now he's gone. He's gone. How could somebody kill my Ronan?"

Ivy looked up at me through her tears and began to sob. *This is the pain she's been avoiding,* I thought. As she continued to cry, she suddenly blurted, "*She* did it!" Her continence quickly changed from sadness to anger.

"Who did what, Ivy?" I calmly asked her.

"That witch of a wife! *She* killed him!"

"She killed him?"

"She didn't love him. She was cold, mean and controlling. He used to tell me about their arguments and the way she treated him."

"How did she treat him?"

"She had money and she never let him forget it. She berated him for not bringing in a steady income. She'd make him ask over and over again for spending money, household money. She loved picking up the check just to make him feel small. But the truth is that she was running out of money and she had a whopping insurance policy on him. She did it."

A myriad of thoughts raced through my mind in what couldn't have been more than a few seconds. I could feel my heart-rate increasing. I was excited to have someone so close to one of the victims in my office, yet I began to have a mini-internal battle.

I looked up at the clock above Ivy's head. *We don't have much time,* I thought. *Do I take advantage of her vulnerable state to dig deeper into Ronan Tate's murder? She's so unguarded right now. It would be so easy to talk about the murder instead of her pain. She's probably got all kinds of stuff to tell. I just want to ask her a few questions. Stop it, Morgan. Just help her. Help her. Trust the process.*

Just then, I felt the sinking despair that can come from delaying gratification and doing the right thing. I made a mental note of what Ivy said about Ronan's wife. I then continued on with the task at hand, helping my client. "It would be awful if his wife did kill him," I said. "But what we do know is that somebody you loved with all your heart is gone, and I'm so sorry."

Ivy began to cry again.

"I'm so sorry that you lost somebody you loved," I continued. "And I can see that you're hurting. But you don't have to suffer alone anymore. You don't have to stifle or suppress your feelings anymore to cope with your pain. The weight from this secret has been lifted. Feel the pain from losing this man that you loved so much. Have your feelings. Cry." Ivy wept aloud for the remainder of the session.

As the session ended, I walked Ms. Carlisle to Kendall's desk. Just then, I noticed Mayor Flint coming in the door. "Kendall, would you please give Ms. Carlisle an appointment for two weeks from today?" I instructed.

"I sure will. Come ovah heah, Ms. Carlisle, and let me set you up for week afta next."

"Mayor Flint?" Ivy said to him as she blinked her eyes, questioning her vision.

"Uhhh—hi," the mayor awkwardly stuttered as he answered Ms. Carlisle.

"Good to see you."

"Uhhh—yes. Good to see you, too."

I watched their awkward interaction, thinking, *He's holding his head down. He is not giving Ivy any eye contact. That's not like Cash. She spoke to him like she knew him. This is Body Language 101. He's nervous— maybe even embarrassed. What's that about? He's one of the most outgoing people I know, and he's the mayor. His odd behavior is about Ivy. He's trying to avoid her.*

"Mr. Mayor, come on in," I said politely. "Hold my calls, Kendall." Mayor Flint practically ran past the super model and Kendall to get into my office. I had to hotfoot it a bit to catch up with him.

"Cash, always good to see you," I said as I entered my office. "Have a seat." He nervously sat down on the couch, pulled a handkerchief from the lapel of his navy-blue Italian suit, and wiped away beaded sweat from his forehead. His discomfort was palpable. "What's going on, Cash?"

"Oh, nothing, Morgan," he anxiously replied. "Told you I'd be stopping by really soon to say hi. This is me stopping by." He laughed.

"Cash, you're sweating. What's going on?"

"It's hot in here. Aren't you hot? Like I said, Morgan, I was in the neighborhood, and I wanted to come by to see your new digs. Show me your office." He scanned the entire office, in validation of his visit.

"Okay, let's go on a tour," I said as I got up and walked toward the door.

"Oh, no, no, no," he interjected. "Ahhhh, I want to know about this *room*. I know there's a lot of history here. Look at that bookcase." He pointed to my bookcase and scrutinized it as if it was the most interesting thing he had ever seen. But I could tell he was really hiding something from Ms. Carlisle. He did not want to risk any more conversation with her. His safety zone, for now, was my office, so I decided to oblige him. For the next ten minutes I provided an extensive history of everything in the four walls that sheltered us, wrapping it up with, "...Now the chair you're sitting in is new. Got it from Crate & Barrel. Okay, Cash. I have a patient coming soon. What's going on?"

His eyes were still nervously active. He glanced at his watch, looked up at me, and slapped both of his thighs a good, resounding smack. "Will ya look at the time?" he said in a hurried tone. "I've got ta get back ta the office, Morgan."

I remained seated, peering at him over my glasses with my arms folded and my chin held up by my right hand. "Call me when you want to talk, Cash." I got up to show him to the door.

As Cash passed Kendall, he seemed to be scanning the reception area, apparently checking to see if the coast was clear. When he noticed that the waiting room was empty, his gait, posture and tone of voice all relaxed. "Goodbye, Ms. Roy, and I'll see you soon, Morgan."

"Okay, Cash," I said as he closed the outer front door.

Kendall and I looked at each other in slight bewilderment. "Well, what was that about, Doc?" she inquired. "He sure didn't stay long."

"No, he didn't Kendall, and I'm not sure why he stopped by."

"Well, I thought it was interestin' that he and Ms. Carlisle knew each othuh. She said they worked out at the same gym togethuh."

"Did she?" I was surprised.

"Yep. She sure did. Oh, my goodness—I just noticed that dirty footprint the mayuh left. I'm gonna have ta try ta clean that up." Kendall pointed to a muddy trail from the front door. As she went off to the bathroom for a paper towel, I walked closer to the grimy mess on the floor. *I've seen that shoeprint before*, I thought. I grabbed my purse, pulled out my cell phone, and took a couple of pictures of Cash's shoeprint.

∽ CHAPTER 8 ∾

"So, accordin' to you and that suspect chart in yo' head, we got a mean, jilted widow, a heartbroken lovah, and now a suspicious mayah who wears the same type o' shoe from the crime scene."

"I know. We got a ways to go. Where are you anyway, Slade? It's nine o'clock at night. What's all that noise in the background?" I was momentarily distracted by the clatters of dishes and the hubbub of loud voices I was hearing from the other end of the phone.

"I'm at Dragos, doin' some of these charbroiled oystahs," Slade said through a mouthful. "You want some o' this? Umf, umf, umf. Too good." I could sense the sheer delight in his voice. "I'm gonna be here fo' awhile. Come on down."

"Well, I kind of..."

"Oh, let me guess. You lookin' at QVC or the shop-'til-you-drop channel, huh? And then you're gonna read some police reports. Am I wrong? Come on. Tell me I'm wrong. Tell me I'm wrong."

"Whatever, Slade." I replied, perusing my surroundings in pathetic agreement with his assessment. I was so comfortable, sitting in the middle of my bed with the remote control in one hand and a police report in the other that it was almost embarrassing.

"Can't say ouch—ya gotta say amen, huh?" Slade continued. "I got a question. How about shuttin' it down, Wintahs, just for a while? Not tonight. I know I gotta give ya some warnin'. But how 'bout next weekend?"

I sat listening and contemplating his words for a stretch.

"You still there, Wintahs?"

"I'm here."

"Whatcha doin' Saturday aftah next, 'round ten a.m.?"

"I don't know. I don't think I have anything out of the ordinary on the calendar. Why?"

"I have two passes for the Bellamy Stables. I'm pickin' you up for nine-thirty a.m. Be ready," he said firmly, but then gently added, "Okay?"

"Okay," I replied, wondering the nature of Slade's offer. I had to admit, though, I was excited at the prospect.

"Great!" he replied with relieved excitement. "Well, I need ta finish wrestlin' with these oystahs. Some of the li'l stinkahs look like they're trying ta escape. Catch ya on the othah side of midnight, Wintahs."

"Bon appétit." I replied.

* * * *

Later that night I was awakened from a deep sleep by the sound of the bluesy piano ringtone of my cell phone. I struggled to straighten the black-rimmed eyeglasses lying crookedly on my face to see the caller ID. "Bryson," I said out loud. I took my glasses off and put the phone down without answering it, hoping sleep would immediately revisit my mind and body. I patiently lay there, waiting for a second chance at hibernation.

But instead of revisiting dreamland, my mind began to sift through the evidence and the suspects, adding and subtracting occurrences and details. I opened my eyes and looked around. The police reports and pictures were spread across my bed. The TV was still streaming in QVC: "Order now, and you can get our lowest price ever."

That's why they're dragging their feet, I suddenly thought. *They've been ordered to.* I slowly began to drift back to sleep, only to be awakened again by my phone. "Dammit, Bryson, I'm not answering this," I shouted. Then, without thought, I found myself pressing the green talk button.

"What do you want, Cole?" I languidly slurred.

"Hello, Morgan," he said in his most cocky, suggestive voice. "You sound like you're in bed."

"What do you want, Cole? I thought I asked you to stop calling me." My stomach began to knot. Suddenly, Maslow scampered out of the bedroom and began to bark at the front door. "Quiet, Maslow, quiet!" I yelled, then turned back to my caller, speaking more resolutely this time: *What do you want, Cole?*

"You always know the answer to that, Morgan. Oh, and if you really wanted me to stop calling, you wouldn't have picked up. You knew it was me on the other end." His words were met with uncomfortable silence. "I have some information for you, about the Audubon murders," Bryson continued. He knew this was the one carrot for which I would sell my sobriety from him for. I was so angry. But I didn't know whom I was angrier with—him or myself. The thought of selling my soul to the devil in order to feed a fetish for solving crimes sickened me. I wanted to hang up, but I didn't. I couldn't. I chose not to.

"What do you have, Cole?" I asked, acquiescing to my weakness.

"Yeah, that's what I thought."

"Oh, just spit it out Cole!" I demanded harshly. I could feel him smirking through the phone, enjoying my beef.

"All right, all right, calm down," he finally said. "One of your victims was last seen at Sacred Heart with Monsignor Keegan the night he was murdered. Very shortly before Allister Dean was murdered, there was an argument. He and Monsignor Keegan were going at it hot and heavy. Dean stormed out."

"What were they arguing about? How do they know each other?" Maslow began to furiously bark at the front door once again. "What's the matter with you, Maslow? Quiet!"

"That's all I'm going to tell you right now," Bryson said. "But if you let me in"—*ding-dong* went my doorbell—"I'll tell you the rest, and oh, so much more."

I bolted to my front door and swung it open in utter disbelief and ire. There he was, on the other side of my black iron gate, silhouetted by the darkness of night. I began to chuckle in exasperated disappointment and indignation as I switched my porch light on.

"Okay," I snapped, "I asked you to lose my number, and you call me on the phone at midnight! I tell you I don't want to see you anymore, and you show up on my doorstep! I'm not doing this anymore, Cole!" I said all of this, sadly realizing I was still trying to convince myself. He moved in closer. I could see his deep-set green eyes and that perfectly chiseled jaw on his six-foot three frame. Maslow began to growl with the animus of a protective pet.

"Open the door, Dr. Winters," Bryson's arrogantly deep voice demanded. I looked down at Maslow as he growled. I looked back up at Cole's smug face. I gazed toward the heavens and thought, *I give up, God. What I'm doing's not working. You're gonna have to do this for me. Please remove this sin from my life.*

"Open the door, Winters," Bryson confidently sang as I turned my gaze back toward him. But this time, when I looked at him, I was no longer fighting my own thoughts. My desires were no longer betraying what I knew to be right. I looked him squarely in the eye, picked Maslow up, shut the door with a slam of affirmation, turned the porch light off, and walked away from the door.

❧ CHAPTER 9 ❧

"Father, forgive me, for I have sinned. It's been five years since my last confession. My heart is heavy with guilt, sadness, shame, and self-loathing," I said as reticence permeated the tiny, somber confessional.

"I am here for you to confess, and with the grace of God, release the sin or sins that brought you here, my child," the cloaked priest responded from the other side.

"Father, forgive me, for I have sinned," I repeated. "It's been five years since my last confession." With a deep breath, grasping for the courage to reveal my ugly secret, I sheepishly mumbled, "I've been sleeping with a married man."

*   *   *   *

The parking lot of Sacred Heart Cathedral was full, but I was determined not to walk in late today. *Dong, dong, dong, dong* went the church bell, informing all that it was noon, and Mass would commence. I scurried into the front door as the greeter handed me a church bulletin. "Good morning, Dr. Winters," he said warmly.

"Good morning," I replied as I looked ahead to hear the choir singing their opening hymn, "Cleanse Me." The priests, altar boys and servers began the processional up the long aisle toward the altar. *Made it*, I said to myself as an usher showed me to an empty seat.

"In the name of the Father and of the Son and of the Holy Spirit," Monsignor Keegan exalted as his baritone voice resounded through the church. The congregation lifted their right hands, touched the middle of their foreheads, then the middle of their chests, and then both shoulders, making the sign of the cross.

"The grace of our Lord Jesus Christ and the love of God and the fellowship of the Holy Spirit be with you all."

"And also with you," the congregation responded in perfunctory unison.

As time passed and we continued to stand, sit, sing, listen, kneel and pray, I fine-tuned my attention to Msgr. Keegan's homily:

"...My friends, as the end of time grows nearer, we must no longer delay the actions of the righteous in the eyes of God: *Amici temporalis inveteratur extremum propius nec diu moremur actiones oportet justum est apud Deum.* Put on your armor of God, so that you will be able to stand and fight the evil of the devil. It is what He would have us do, in that we *must* do as He says. We *must* do as ordered. *Ad Deum appropinquare , et appropinquare tibi. Tersus manus peccatores et mundo corde qui omnes duplices:* Draw close to God, and he will draw close to you. Clean your hands, sinners, and clean your hearts, all you who are double-minded. Come close to God, and He will come close to you. Recognize that you are *sinners*, get your soiled hands clean, wavering individuals with divided interests, and clean yourselves of your adultering spirits." He paused and looked around.

"I want you to realize that we are at *war*. We must *purge* ourselves and this world of sin. We are at war against the liars, the cheaters, the backstabbers, the thieves, the evildoers, and we must be prepared and willing to do the work of the righteous to right these wrongs. *'Dabit Dominus inimicos tuos qui consurgunt adversum te corruentes in conspectu tuo per unam viam venient contra te et per septem fugient a facie tua':* The Lord will bring forth our enemies, that make themselves known against thee, and they will perish. They will come in once as your foe, and leave seven different ways fleeing. *Video autem aliam legem in membris meis repugnantem legi mentis meae et captivantem me in lege peccati quae est in membris meis. Infelix ego homo quis me liberabit de corpore mortis huiu:* Sad men and women that we are. Who is going to bring us from this place called death? My brothers and sisters, this is where peace lies. This is where peace lies."

Msgr. Keegan's apocalyptically impressive sermon drew to a close. Mass was over. Churchgoers were either leaving or greeting each other.

"Hi, Dr. Winters," "Hi, Dr. Winters," one parishioner after another greeted me.

"Hi, good morning," I said, shaking their hands in reply and premeditatively moving through the crowd. I wanted to talk to the Monsignor. I wasn't the only one, though. He was surrounded. But I continued to meet and greet people through the feeder bands of people until I came face to face with my subject.

"Good morning, Monsignor." I said, smiling and extending my hand.

"Good morning, Dr. Winters," he responded genially as he shook my hand with his familiarly firm grip. "Good to see you here on a Sunday morning."

"So glad to have a chance to talk to you, Monsignor. That was quite a sermon." *Quite a depressingly heavy sermon,* I was thinking.

"Why, thank you, Doctor."

"You're welcome. When I think about it, preparation for death is something we can look at in so many different ways. But your blunt, fact-filled, and not to mention Latin take on the subject was enlightening, to say the least."

"I must thank you again, Dr. Winters, for your words of acknowledgment. It has been a spell since we've had a good chat. How have you been?" He had a hint of levity in his voice.

"I'm good, Monsignor. I just have so much going on these days. How have you been?"

"Indeed, Doctor, I can't turn the TV on these days without seeing your face."

"Yeah, I'd kind of like some of that to go away. In fact, can I ask you about something completely apart from that?"

"Why, certainly."

"Well, a friend of mine asked me if I knew anything about collecting guns. She wants to start collecting. And I guess because of all the work I've been doing with the police department, she thought I might have a clue. But I don't. I don't know anything about guns. But, as I'm standing here talking to you, I remembered that you have a rather extensive gun collection, right?"

The Monsignor responded by summoning his guarded demeanor as he folded his arms, furrowed his brow, and nodded in the affirmative. But I continued to ask questions as if there were no interruption in his comfort.

"Where did you start? What was your first gun?"

He paused in what seemed to be suspicious reflection before sharing. "Well, I started with the Colt Dragoon. It's a beautifully crafted handgun dating back to 1848. She might want to see if she could get her hands on one of those. That's where I would start."

"Okay. What other types of handguns do you have?"

"Well I have a Derringer, and a—" He paused again and digressed from the topic. "Who is this friend of yours, Doctor?"

"Oh, just an old college buddy."

"Well why don't you ask your old college buddy to give me a call? I certainly don't want to bore you with all of this."

"Oh, no, Monsignor. You're not boring me."

"You're too kind, Doctor. Tell your friend to give me a call—or, better yet, the best advice I can give is for her to Google it. There's oodles of information one can find on the Internet, about anything these days," the clergyman summarily and rather impassively concluded, letting me know that my fact-finding mission was over...or was it?

"You are absolutely right," I said. "There is so much information out there in cyberspace." I had a thought and peered over the Monsignor's shoulder. "I think I see Commander Slade over there. He and I need to talk about those uptown murders."

"You're helping out with the uptown murders?" the Monsignor inquired as he tilted his head forward.

"Yes, I am, Monsignor."

"Such a pity. They all seem to have been such upstanding members of the community."

"Yeah, it's been quite a heartbreaking challenge sifting through all the minutiae of information. But we have some new information about one of the victims, and we're hoping it's going to lead us closer to the killer or killers."

"Well, that's excellent, Doctor. Now, did I hear you correctly? Did you say that you have information on the killer?" The Monsignor's eyes grew more round with what seemed to be intense curiosity. *Ah, ha!* I thought. *There it is—a break in his reserve. His comportment took an anxious shift.*

"Yes, hopefully we do," I replied.

"Do you think you know who it is?" he boldly asked with a tad more fervor.

"You know that's all part of it, Monsignor. The leads are really good." *Okay, what the heck,* I thought. *I'm just gonna ask him.* "Did you know Mr. Dean, Monsignor? He lived so close to the church. I was just wondering if by any chance you knew him. Allister Dean?"

The Monsignor seemed surprised by my question. I was reminded of my 'Interviewing Techniques' class, where I was taught that the basic rule of thumb is not to be afraid of the quiet in conversation when waiting for a reply. Patience in that moment can yield a treasure, if you'll let it. So I stood there, patiently waiting for the Monsignor's reply. He took a deep breath, looked into my eyes, and began to speak.

"Mr. Dean was..."

"Hi Monsignor," said an excited white-bonneted little old lady, cutting into our conversation. "I just wanted to shake your hand and thank you for the fine Mass this morning. And it looks like I'm going to be able to shake the hand of *the* famous Dr. Morgan Winters as well. Today's my lucky day." We exchanged pleasantries with the parishioner. And, just like that, that moment in time was gone. The conversation was over. Monsignor Keegan seemed relieved.

"As always, so good to see you, Dr. Winters," he said. "Take care now." I watched him proceed through the eager crowd of parishioners.

❧ CHAPTER 10 ❧

Ding-dong went the doorbell as Maslow began barking.

"Quiet, Maslow, quiet! *Coming!*" I yelled as I stumbled to the door with one boot on, the other in my hand.

"Arf! Arf! Arf!" my dog continued to yap as I opened the door.

"Where ya at, Wintahs?" It was Slade. I was always surprised by the almost Pavlovian response of comfort that came from hearing Slade ask me, "Where ya at?" It rendered me pleasantly distracted from my own thoughts.

"As you can see, Slade, I'm kind of ready," I told him cheerfully. "I need a few more minutes, though. Come on in. You remember your buddy Maslow?" I looked down at my delirious dog, who was starting to jump at my guest. "Down, Maslow, down! Let him in!"

Slade casually stepped inside the doorway and immediately began to converse with Maslow warmly and affectionately. "Hey, boy. Come to Jackson. How ya doin'? How ya doin'? Aww, I know, I know."

Look at 'em, I thought as I pulled on my other boot. I couldn't tell which one was having more fun as Slade playfully asked my dog, "Who wants kisses? Who wants kisses?"

After they finished their frolic, Slade walked over to the front door, out of my eyeshot. Then he walked over to the plush red sofa I was sitting on in the den. He had both hands behind his back. He stood there looking at me with his familiar devilish grin.

"Okay, Slade, I know that look. What are you up to? What's behind your back?"

"Not up to anything, Wintahs. Just tryin' to visualize."

"Visualize what?"

"Visualize how you're gonna look wearing this!" He presented a sleek gray leather cowboy hat from behind his back.

"What's this?" I asked, surprised.

"Whadd'ya mean, 'What's this?' It's a hat! Here." He placed it on my head.

"I know it's a hat, Slade," I replied, taking it off to get a better look at it.

"Mine's in the truck. Gotta have one of these when you're ridin' horses, ya know?"

I looked at the hat with a smile of appreciation. I then made my way to the mirror over the fireplace, put the hat back on, and jauntily tilted it to the side. I could see the reflection of Slade's pride-filled grin in the mirror as he stood behind me.

"You're looking awfully proud of yourself," I said to his reflection as his smile morphed into a boyish blush.

"Whatever, Wintahs. Let's roll." Slade gave the mirror one more gaze before making his way to the door.

* * * *

It was a beautiful day. The sun was shining, and the air was almost crisp as we drove along the neighborhoods and highways of New Orleans to reach our destination.

"So you're tellin' me Bryson told ya that Monsignor Keegan not only *knew* Allister Dean, but that they argued the night he was murdered?" Slade inquired aggressively. "How come we didn't know 'bout this? And what's Bryson doin' tellin' ya 'bout it?"

I shrugged my shoulders in feigned ignorance.

"I know, I know," he continued. "One day I'm gonna learn. People tell ya things they don't tell other people. But Bryson? What's *really* goin' on here? I'm thinkin' me and the boss need ta have a sit-down Monday morning."

"Really?" I casually asked. "You think so?"

"Yeah, I do."

I momentarily sat in contemplation. *Slade's questions and my information only invite more concern, no real answers. In fact, the one question I could answer, I wasn't going to.*

The last thing I want is for Slade to find out about my relationship with Cole. I know it's over, but I hate that it happened. It's my secret. You know better, Morgan. You know all about the personal and collateral damage that can come from secrets. You're a shrink. But it's a hard pill to swallow when it's my *secret.*

You can't let this shame, guilt, or fear be your point of reference anymore. I'm not going to let my fear of Slade or anybody finding out about my affair govern how I do this.

"So you're going into Bryson's office when we get back, huh?" I finally asked Slade. "I think that's a good idea. We don't really know how much Bryson knows. We just don't know. But what we do know is that Bryson has a long history of being a shrewd, hands-on and involved administrator, when it serves him. But when it doesn't, he can hamper an investigation like nobody else. He knows more. You said it yourself. He's been apathetic throughout most of the probe. Then he leaks this info to me."

"Sittin' still's not workin' for him anymore," Slade chimed in.

"Maybe it never worked for him."

"What do you mean?"

"Maybe somebody's forcin' 'im to keep things quiet. We don't really know how high the cover-up goes— the chief? The mayah? And yeah, I said it—*cover-up*."

"Maybe."

"All right, all right, enough about this. We got about an hour left o' this ride. I'm gonna lay down some ground rules."

"Oh, really?"

"Yeah, 'really.' First, no more talkin' 'bout murder victims, their families, their friends, their enemies, their jobs, their cars, their mammas, their daddies, their hair, their toenails. You feel me?"

"Uh-huh."

"Second, no talkin' about any of those people we work with, either—the mayah, the superintendent, his deputy, the deputy's secretary, the mayah's wife, the mayah's dog, his aunt or his uncle. You with me, Wintahs?" We bumped fists. "And last, but certainly not least, we're gonna have some *fun!* Okay? Whad'ya know about *this*?"

Slade reached into his glove compartment for a CD, popped it into the player, and turned up the volume. A throbbing familiar baseline started to play as Slade began to bop his head back and forth to the beat and sing along:

> *"I said a hip hop,*
> *The hipping and the hopping, stop, a rocking*
> *To boogie, and feel the boogie,*
> *To boogie and feel the rhythm.*
> *Now, what you hear is all for real—Slade's rappin' to the sounds,*
> *And me, Winters, and my friends are gonna try to have some fun.*
> *See, I am Jackson Slade, and I'd like to say what's up, Morgan...*

"Come on, Wintahs, you know this!" he said as he handed me an imaginary microphone. "Come on, Wintahs, take the mike!"

I looked at him with amused curiosity as I reluctantly began to 'sing along': *"But first, I gotta sing along, sing along to the song that makes you dance, say jump up and boogie to the music."*

Slade joined in: *"Let's jam, and don't stop, jam the beats that you wanna hear...."* We both enjoyed a hearty laugh as we finished singing the tune.

"Remembah when we first met, Wintahs?" he suddenly asked me.

"Like it was yesterday."

"Prove it."

"What?"

"Prove it."

"We met at the trial of Boudreaux Dupré, the Beignet King. Two months after the acquittal of Mr. Dupré, I was in my office a little earlier than usual reviewing patient notes when the phone rang. " 'Dr. Winters' Office,' " I said, mocking myself answering the phone in my sweetest angelic voice. " 'May I speak to Doctah Wintahs?' " I continued, doing my impression of Slade in a deep southern drawl. " 'This is she,' " I said sweetly, batting my eyes. " 'Doctah Wintahs, this is Commandah Jackson Slade with the NOPD. I don't know if you remembah me, but we met during the Beignet King trial. I interviewed you right afta his wife was killed.' " " 'Oh yes, of course, I remember you, Commander. How can I help you?' "

The more story I told, the deeper my southern accent got. " 'First thing you can do for me is ta call me Jackson.' " " 'Okay, Jackson. And please call me Morgan. That was an easy one. What else can I help you with?' " " 'Well, Dr. Winters, I mean Morgan, the Superintendent was so impressed with your testimony durin' that trial he asked me to get in touch with ya. We'd like to use your expertise on some of the cases we're workin' on.' " " 'So, what exactly *would* working with the NOPD entail, Mr. Detective?'—oh, that's right, 'Jackson.' "

By this time, Slade and I could hardly contain our laughter. "That's pretty good, Wintahs."

"Do I remember! Before there was a *Doctor* Winters, there was a little girl wanting to be *Detective* Winters.

So I really was thrilled with the idea of helping out the NOPD, even before I knew any of the details."

"What changed? What made you stop wanting to be a cop?"

"I got older, and the dream of wanting to catch people that did bad things got replaced with wanting to know *why* people did bad things. Do you remember that first case?"

"LeJune Tayor, shot four times in the back, lyin' face down on the pavement in front of Eddie's restaurant," Slade quickly answered, again diverting his attention from the road to momentarily lock eyes with me. "And the first thing he wanted me ta do was bring ya over ta meet with Haddock."

We smiled in unison with a flash of amusement and attraction. I broke our eye contact to see a daredevil squirrel crossing the road. "Slade! A squirrel!" I exclaimed, pointing ahead. He swerved, barely missing the cute rodent.

"Good call, Wintahs. Don't have time for a funeral on this trip. Rocky lives ta see anothah day—well maybe not a day, but *I* didn't kill him. Okay, here we are." He pulled into the stables as a man in blue jeans, a blue plaid shirt and a big white cowboy hat came over to us.

"Mornin', Commanda," he said to Slade.

"Mornin', Zach," Slade responded.

"See ya brought some company. Mornin', ma'am," he greeted me, then turned back to Slade. "You know the drill, Commanda. Pull in over there behind the barn, and we'll get y'all checked in. See y'all inside."

"Yuh ready for this, Wintahs?" Slade asked as we pulled in behind the red barn.

"Nope, but I'm doing it anyway," I replied as we had one more chuckle before donning my new cowgirl hat on and stepping out of Slade's truck.

We checked in, and Zach took us to our horses. Slade had a magnificently exquisite black horse named Panther. I was given a charming, mostly white-and-brown beauty named Chloe. I listened carefully as Slade took his time showing me how to mount and give commands to Chloe. By the end of my lesson, I was confident in nothing. Horseback riding involved a degree of letting go, relinquishing control, surrendering. I wasn't there yet.

"You good, Wintahs?"

"Do I look like I'm good?"

Slade looked at me, twisting his mouth to the side, and then bursting into laughter. "You're good, Wintahs, you're good. Haaaa!" he commanded his horse as we began to ride.

As we rode, I began to relinquish control and trust in the moment. Chloe was strong, but gentle. She was a joy. She was just what the doctor ordered. We rode through open fields, shallow waters, and at times almost jungle-like areas, enjoying the peaceful, natural rhythm of riding a horse.

Midway through the trail, we stopped for a lunch Slade had packed away in his saddle. He covered a small patch of grass in an open field with an old gray blanket and invited me to have a seat. He then set a bottle of white wine, two plastic cups, and two ham sandwiches on the blanket. He stood there, looking at the setting with that familiar pride-filled grin. *"Bam!"* he exclaimed as he placed the last item on the blanket.

I was impressed and amused as I smiled back at him. "Sit down, Slade," I affectionately requested. "This is pretty cool. In fact, this is awesome."

He could hardly contain himself as he continued to smile while opening the bottle of wine. He knew he had managed to really impress his friend. We relaxed in the open field. I found myself sinking into a deeper level of emotional comfort.

"I gotta tell ya, Slade. This has been so much fun. In fact, it's been a while since I've had this much fun. Thank you. We have to..." Suddenly, my train of thought was interrupted by Slade's easy good looks. I looked away to gather my thoughts.

"We have ta *what,* Wintah's?"

"We have to do this again. Right?" I looked back at him, only to be more taken by the masculine warmth his eyes exuded.

"Right!" He smiled as the light from the sun seemed to sit between us. He looked even deeper into my eyes. "I'm having fun too, Morgan, and we will do this again." He leaned over and gently placed a kiss on my cheek. I could smell the remnants of his aftershave as he pulled away. I was overwhelmed by the fragrance.

"I had a talk with Monsignor Keegan on Sunday," I said, going back to business.

"Really?" Slade replied.

"Yeah, I point-blank asked him if he knew Mr. Dean after he point-blank asked me if I knew who the killer was."

Slade briefly turned away from me to take a sip of wine. "What happened? What'd he say?"

"He didn't answer me. He was on the verge of telling me something when a parishioner interrupted us, killing the moment. It was over after that. He clammed up. He knew Allister Dean, and I do believe he was with him the night he was killed."

"I know the feelin'," Slade mumbled.

"What was that?" I quickly asked.

"Ahh, nothing, Wintahs." He was clearly growing frustrated. He didn't like the higher-ups blocking the investigation—*his* investigation. He took it personally. Nor did he like my bringing up the murders again. The mood was broken. "Ready to get back to the ranch?" he asked, extending his hand to help me up.

"Ready." I said as I put my hand in his and we got on our horses and rode back.

⊰ CHAPTER 11 ⊱

As I walked past Superintendent Bryson's door on my way to Slade's office, Slade's voice stopped me in my tracks. I listened intently.

"I'm goin' to bring Monsignor Keegan in for questioning," I heard him tell Bryson.

"Whoa, slow down there, Commander," Bryson calmly responded. "What's all this about?"

"What's all this about? No disrespect, Superintendent, but you *know* what this is about. I know you're aware of Keegan being with Allister Dean the night he was murdered, and I'm pretty certain that you know more. So it's just what I said. I'm gonna bring him in, and then take matters into my own hands."

"Take matters into your own hands?" Bryson asked incredulously.

"Yeah, meaning I'm gonna do whatever I hafta do ta find out who's killin' people in uptown New Orleans."

"Really? And how do you *know* Allister Dean was with Monsignor Keegan the night he was murdered?"

"Come on, boss. Let's not play aroun'. You know somethin's up here. We have four murdahs, and nobody's liftin' a fingah ta lay any of 'em ta rest but me. Yet I get the feelin' we're moments away from somebody tellin' me to say, 'Case closed.' These aren't random crimes. What's the deal? We've been here before. We know the drill. What's so different?"

"Sit down, Slade."

I assumed Slade acquiesced to Bryson's request.

"Listen, I don't like what's been going on any more than you do," Bryson continued. "A while back, Flint comes into my office and not so passively mandates that we close these cases ASAP—not investigate, but *close*. I was given no rhyme or reason. I figure he's up for re-election, if you know what I mean, and he just wants all of this to go away. I'm frustrated, too. You know me, Slade. This is *not* how I do business."

"I get why you leaked the information then, but what do *I* do?" Slade asked helplessly. "Files are missing. It's like hell tryin' ta get a warrant or a subpoena. What do I do?"

Dead silence suddenly filled the office.

"Where is she?" Bryson finally demanded.

"Where is who, boss?"

"Don't play with me, Slade. Where is she?" My heart began to pound. I was certain he was asking about me.

"Ahh, no jokes here," Slade responded curtly. "Who you talkin' 'bout? What the hell are you talkin' about?"

"Don't play with me, Slade. I'm going to ask you one more time: *Where—is—she?*"

"Who?"

"I know she's in on this with you. You're screwing her, aren't you? *Aren't you?*"

As tension-filled quiet permeated the walls, suddenly I heard someone's phone ring, which I believe snapped Bryson out of his fit. In a calmer voice he went on to say. "So, ahhh, if the two of you, you and Dr. Winters, can extricate a real murderer out of all of this, by all means do it. So bring Keegan in. Do whatever you have to. But if you tell anyone I gave you the green light, I'll deny it and throw you under a bus so fast you won't know what hit you. Got it?"

"Got it," I heard Slade meekly reply.

Sensing that conversation had ended, I scurried away from Bryson's office and made my way to Slade's, to deal with the fallout.

*   *   *   *

I peered through the blinds, focusing on a silhouette of a man walking down the sterile, white-walled precinct corridor. *Yep, that's him,* I thought. *I don't know what to say to him.* His face was serious, but he was still too far away for me to infer how angry he was. What I did know, knowing Slade, was that he *was* irate. I could feel the anticipation and fear seething inside of me as I sat down in a chair under the window I had been peering through. The door slowly opened as Slade entered. He was in such deep thought he didn't notice me sitting in his office.

"Slade. Hey. How'd it go?" I asked, pretending I hadn't heard his contentious exchange with Bryson.

Slade slowly turned around and gave me a half-hearted smile. "Oh, hey," he said. "Didn't see ya theah."

"Well, how'd it go?"

He took a seat behind his desk. "Just as we thought," he said. "We've only been scratchin' the surface. I think he told me everything he knows, but I'm not positive. Too bad you couldn't 'a' been theah."

He gave me little or no eye contact. His brows were bunched. He scratched his forehead over and over again. When I did see his eyes, they were thought-filled, not focused. His facial expressions were full of annoyance, confusion, tension. Clearly he was hurt.

"Talk to me." I asked.

He turned toward me, looking completely bewildered. My heart sank. At that moment I knew Slade had completely figured it out. He knew about my affair with Bryson.

"Let's go for a ride, Slade," I offered.

"No, I think we're good heah," he calmly replied.

"Okay, Slade. I know we usually go to the cathedral, but you know that's off limits for a while because of the Monsignor, so if you don't want to go for a ride, then spill it. I'm not doing the silent treatment. Either we go for a ride and you talk to me, or you talk to me right now about what happened in there with Bryson."

He thought for a moment. "Let's go for a ride? I'll drive," he finally consented as we gathered our belongings and headed out.

The air outside was thick, heavy, and uncomfortable. It was the same in Slade's air-conditioned truck as we drove through the first few red lights without a word between us. *He knows,* I thought as my shame-filled secret began to direct my mind toward fear. *I don't care,* was the next lie I told myself as self-righteous anger began to swell inside of me. *He's either going to talk to me, or I'm out of here.* I was running hot and cold.

But before I could conjure up any more fear-based reflection, he interrupted me. "Beautiful day, ain't it, Wintahs?" he said with pseudo cheer. "Sun shinin' bright, no clouds, jus' kinda hot and sticky, like it usually is, though, right? Good ta get out every once in a while. Know what I mean?"

"Yeah, I know what you mean," I responded, relieved for the moment. "Enough about the damn weather, Slade. You and I don't beat around the bush. That's why we work. You've been acting strange since you came back from seeing Bryson. Talk to me. Tell me what went on in there. Tell me *everything.*" I said, as I pulled my sunglasses off.

Slade slowly maneuvered the car into a parking area at City Park, and turned the engine off. We sat, facing a duck-filled lagoon. "Well, Wintahs," he began, "the superintendent told me the mayah told him to make the murdahs go away." He paused for a moment. "Oh, he also asked me if I was screwin' you. I kinda wanna ask *you* the same question about him though, ya know? But I think I already know the answer to that. Don't I?"

I could feel my heart rate increase as I leaned back into the seat and sarcastically chuckled at Slade's question. Again, we sat in uncomfortable silence. But this time, there was no wondering why. I thought to respond in anger to his not-so-subtle jab, but instead I took a deep breath and paused. *You have no one to blame for this but yourself,* I thought. I then opened my window to get a better look at a young couple slowly paddling through the murky lagoon water. *What a beautiful day,* I thought. *The sun's shining. The birds are chirping. How could such a lovely day be a part of such a malaise? Doesn't seem right. Oh, I get it God. There's a sun shining over most rocks. But you have to come out from hiding under the rock in order to see or feel it, right? So, I guess this is me coming out from hiding under this rock of deception I've created. Geez, I'm starting to sound like Mother Franklin.*

"Look, Slade," I finally told him. "I didn't want you to find out like this. And, yeah, if I had my druthers, this was something I would have loved to have taken to my grave. But that's not what was supposed to happen. That's not what happened."

"Hey, what you do, and with whom—did I say that right?" he interrupted. "With whom you do it with is none of my business. You don't owe me any explanations, Wintahs. We're just friends, right?" He turned to face me. "The two of us, me and you, create this grand plan ta tackle deception and crime. Ha, that's funny now. Anyway, as you know, first thing this mornin' I walk into Bryson's office, and *bam!* Ya know, it just caught me off guard." He shook his head and displayed a faint smile, masking his obvious hurt.

"And you're right," I retorted. "I don't owe you any explanation, but I want to give you one. Yes, I did have a relationship with Bryson. But I ended it. It's over. That's why he's so angry."

Slade gazed into my eyes as if he was reaching for something to undo his disappointment. All I could offer, though, was the ugly truth. "Like I said, Wintahs," he quipped, "you don't owe me anythin'. What you do is your business."

"Yeah, right. What I do *is* my business when I'm the only one involved. But I'm not the only one involved here. I was doing what I see my patients do all the time: evade, avoid, suppress, and ultimately mess up in a ball of hurt. And I messed up big-time. I not only hurt myself, but I hurt other people, too. I hurt *you*. I didn't just hurt you, but I'm afraid I've lost your trust. And for that I am truly sorry, and I will work to repair it."

I gently rested my hand on top of his. My eyes began to glisten with tears as I tilted my head to the side, capturing his glance. "Slade, you're the last person I want to hurt or lose trust from," I told him.

In that moment I noticed a warm smile of relief overcome his face as he looked away, fighting back tears himself. Even though, as a shrink, I know tears are cleansing, at times I still found them difficult to express. Slade did as well.

We waved back at a group of adolescents who were innocently waving at us as they were being ushered through the park. I seized the opportunity to discreetly emancipate one of the tears I had been holding onto.

CHAPTER 12

"So, Doc, you tellin' me that Commanda' Slade met with Superintendent Bryson and he said the mayor told him ta' make the murdahs go away? Now, ain't that somethin'! Well, who gave him the right ta do that? Lawd, I remember the last time somebody told *me* ta go away. And I know, Doc, it's a li'l different from those murdahs, but trust me. It's the same principle. It was Jimmy Delsalva. He lived back o' town over theah by that po'boy shop. Oh, you know which one I'm talkin' 'bout. Come on, Doc. Which one is it? You know, back o' town?"

I shrugged my shoulders and shook my head, letting Kendall know I had no idea which of the many po'boy shops she was talking about. But she insisted, as she looked at me, waiting for a name. She eventually went on.

"Anyway, he wanted me ta go away, because he didn't want somebody there tellin' the truth on him. I saw him stealin'. And ya know me, Doc. I try ta always tell the truth. What's that Mother Franklin used to say, 'The truth might sting like a bee, but in the end, it's gonna set you free.' " Kendall paused, looked toward the sky in honor of dear ol' Mother Franklin, and then jumped right back into the conversation.

"But you know what, Doc? I didn't go away. I stayed right theah, and I told the truth. Yes, I did and Jimmy Desalva was set free with that truth. Yes, indeed, he was. His soul was set free with the truth, but the rest of him went ta jail. He didn't quite see it the way I did, though—hear him tell it. Go on, Doc, I interrupted you. You were saying that Superintendent Bryson was spillin' the beans ta Commanda Slade."

"There's also another piece to the puzzle."

"What is it, Doc? Don't leave me hangin'."

"Not what is it, but *who* is it? Monsignor Keegan." Kendall's eyes got so wide I could almost see her pupils dilating in excitement.

"Monsignor Keegan?" she blurted in disbelief. "What you say, Doc! Go 'way from here! I know Monsignor ain't exactly the warmest or friendliest man of God out there, but, oh, Lawd, what could he have ta do with these murders, Doc?"

"Remember Allister Dean, the man killed in Audubon Place?"

"Yeah."

"Well, come to find out, the Monsignor was the last person to see him alive, according to the coroner's estimated time of death, but for some reason he's never been interviewed by anyone. In fact, it's not even in any of the reports."

"Really? Monsignor Keegan? He couldn't 'ave had anything ta do with all o' this. Lawd have mercy."

"Yeah, I know. We just need to keep on digging."

*   *   *   *

I had just seen my last patient for the day and was hunched over my desk, intensely surveying a mountain of paperwork, when Kendall opened the door and peeped her head in. "Don't you stay heah too late now, Doc, okay?" she said. "I'm on my way out. I'm gonna lock the front door."

"I won't," I said. "Have a good evening, and I'll see you in the morning." I was cynically turning pages of the reports Slade had given me. *This is a joke,* I thought. *These reports are missing so much information. I almost feel like I'm wasting my time. You know what, Morgan? You are. This door is closed. I need to go in another way. The truths are going to have to come from somewhere else.*

I shoved the pile of papers away, leaned back in my chair, put my feet up on my desk and closed my eyes. As I often instruct my patients to do when their minds are cluttered with impatient frustration, I slowly inhaled, imagining my mind and body being filled with cloud-like peace. I then exhaled as I envisioned the dark blue smoke of anxiety leaving my frame. I did this several times until internal calm was restored.

"Cash!" I said out loud, as I put my feet on the floor and sat up. *Why was he so uncomfortable the last time he was here? I thought. Hell, why did he really come here? He wanted to tell me something, but he didn't. Why did he tell Bryson to make everything go away? Why was he so uncomfortable with Ivy?*

I grabbed my phone and placed a call to Slade. *Dang it, voicemail.* "Hey, Slade. I got a hunch. I'm going to the mayor's office, and hopefully he'll see me. I'll talk to you later." I took a quick glance at my watch, put my shoes on, grabbed my purse and headed for the door.

❧ CHAPTER 13 ❧

"The Mayor will see you now, Dr. Winters. Follow me."

Cash Flint's secretary, Liz, led me down the long corridor to the mayor's office, where I had never been, though I had been to City Hall many times. The outer office's carpet was a thick, dingy navy-blue. The mahogany-paneled walls were lined with portraits of former mayors. As we reached the oversized mahogany door leading to Cash's office, I turned around and took another look at the outer office. I was almost entranced by what I saw and felt. The air was thick with history and power. Liz opened the door, and there he was, sitting behind his desk, entranced by something in one of his drawers.

"Mr. Mayor? Dr. Winters is here to see you." He seemed to be startled by her voice, the way he quickly closed the drawer and looked up.

"Morgan. Hi. Come on in. Thank you, Liz." She politely smiled and closed the door.

"Hello, Cash," I said. "I decided to take you up on your offer to stop by."

"Well, I'm so glad ya did," he responded as he came toward me with open arms. His embrace was full but vacuous. He was clearly distracted. "To what do I owe the pleasure? Like I said, not that you need an excuse to come by. Here, have a seat." He gestured toward one of two chairs in front of his desk. He sat on the front edge of his desk, maintaining the old one-up Cash Flint position. No matter what, Cash always liked sitting just a little higher than whomever it was he happened to be talking to.

"How are Joyce and the kids?" I asked him. "I saw her at the flea market the other day. Did she tell you?"

"Yes, she did." We sat, smiling at each other for a quick awkward moment. "Now, Morgan, I know you didn't come all this way to tell me you saw Joyce at the flea market. How can I help you?"

"You are absolutely right, Cash. Well, you know I'm helping the police with the Audubon murders. And I'm just not getting anywhere with the reports."

"Oh, I can't believe that, Morgan."

"Cash, somebody's trying to keep us away from the evidence. The reports are full of holes."

"Well, that's just awful. But what do *I* have to do with any of this?"

"I got to thinking that I'm not going to be able to flush out the killer through my usual combing through the reports. I'm just going to have to start talking to people. And that thought lead me straight to you."

"Me?"

"Yep. I was confused about a couple of things. And I thought to myself, 'Why don't you just ask Cash?' So here I am."

"Well, I don't know what I could tell you that would help, but you've got my full attention. I'm all-ears." Cash sat down in the chair next to me, leaned in, looked me in the eye, and turned on his narcissistic charm. He was no longer distracted. "Talk to me," he said with a smile as I simpered in circumspect reciprocation.

I looked away, and then right back into his eyes. "Cash, how do you know Ivy Carlisle?" I began.

He immediately sat back in his chair, crossed his legs, and commandingly folded his arms. An overt wall of protection had suddenly been erected before him. I had to remember, though, that a person like Cash always kept a wall of defense in place at some level. He was a master at making you believe otherwise. But this time, he wasn't able to hide it. *Look at him,* I thought. *Those big blue eyes are betraying him. He's spooked. He's afraid, and would love to flee this conversation, but something's keeping him here.*

"You came over here to ask me *that,* Dr. Winters?" Cash condescendingly asked as he pressed his lips together in agitation. "She's a super model. Everybody knows Ms. Carlisle."

"Oh, okay, it just seemed like you knew each other personally. There's one more thing though," I said. He rolled his eyes in exasperation. I looked down at his feet in relief, noticing he was wearing the same shoes he had worn to my office.

"Make it quick, Morgan. I have things I need to take care of."

"Just this one more thing. It seems as though we found shoe prints from the Dean estate just like the ones you're wearing. They're very unique. I think the name is Forzieri or something like that? Italian right? I asked as Cash sat there stoned faced.

"Cash, did you know Allister Dean?"

He sat there, looking at me. I took a chance. Sometimes it's good to throw everything and see what sticks. But sometimes you throw everything and you get thrown out of the mayor's office. I braced myself for being thrown out. But he continued to just sit and watch my every move. So I gave into the uncomfortable silence by allowing it to be. He then looked up at the ceiling, leaned back in his oversized office chair, angrily shook his head, and mumbled, "Why? Why?" His posture went from defensive to overtly angry. He clenched his fists and pounded the arms of the chair he was sitting in. "Why? Why? Why?"

"Why *what*, Cash?" I gently probed, hoping I hadn't spoken too soon. Again, we sat in silence as the mayor's breathing grew heavier.

"I know Ivy Carlisle because we go to the same gym, and—" The mayor paused as he took another deep breath and exhaled.

"And what, Cash?" I calmly asked.

"You just wait, Morgan. Just wait. You're gonna get what you came here for. Just wait!"

I sat, anticipating his reply.

"I've worked so hard for all of this," he continued in a rather defensive tone. "I've worked so hard for this city. I love being the mayor. I built up that convention center and the civic center, the theater of performing arts. I built all of that. They were falling apart. My predecessors were gonna let 'em all go to hell. I fought 'em. I fought 'em all and I won. Nobody took care of the people like I did. I loved 'em. And they loved me. I'm sure there are a few people in this world that might have been able to do what I've done. Haven't met any of 'em yet though. Not a one. This was my playground. All he had to do was to keep his stupid mouth shut. That's all he had to do. That's all he had to do."

Silence filled the air again as Cash took a deep, pained swallow. "I can't do this anymore," he said plaintively. "It's over."

"You can't do what? *What's* over, Cash?"

His shoulders slumped. His face became sad and drawn. "I knew Ivy Carlisle because we went to the same gym together and she knew." Cash said as he paused to swallow.

"She knew what?"

"She knew that Allister Dean, was my lover."

"Oh, Cash!" I reached for his hand. He pulled away with a look of shame and anger.

"No!" he snapped. "I don't want your sympathy, or whatever it is you're peddling right now, Morgan! Don't touch me! *Don't touch me!*" He wiped his forehead in consternation. "I haven't been sleeping much! You think you might be able to give me something?" Massaging his temples, he looked confused, desolate, shattered. His eyes grew dark, and his speech became erratic.

"Look at this, Morgan. I waited to be fifty-eight years old to start biting my nails. They bleed most days." He looked at his nails and began to laugh. "Oh, I know that look. You're not the only one that can read body language, Dr. Winters. I know what you're thinking. Let's see. Cash isn't doing too well right now. Cash needs help. Cash is sad. Cash, Cash, *Cash, Cash! Would you just shut up, Morgan! Shut the hell up!*"

As his rage mounted, he lifted his head and began to laugh and proclaim, "No, I don't *need* help! There is absolutely nothing wrong with me! *You're* the one with the problem, Morgan. That's right. You have a problem. Just like Allister, you just couldn't leave well enough alone. Because now I *cannot* let you tell *anybody* about this, just like I couldn't let my dear, sweet Allister tell anyone! He was the sweetest, most beautiful man I'd ever seen. I was so happy. But he just couldn't leave well enough alone."

Another wave of sadness and despair came over Cash as he slowly began to sob. He then wiped the tears from his eyes and sat at his desk. He opened one of the drawers and removed a bottle of liquor and a shot glass and placed them on his desk. He then opened another drawer—the one he was looking into when I had walked into his office. He removed a shiny black revolver. He held the gun in one hand and the bottle of spirits in the other as he opened the bottle an poured himself a drink. He grimaced with each shot as he poured himself another and another, only stopping briefly to scratch the side of his head with the barrel of the gun. At this point I was torn between wanting to escape, helping a man in distress, or knowing the rest of the story.

"Cash, what are you doing?" I said. "None of this is that bad. Put the gun down." He went on talking and drinking as if I hadn't said a word.

"Chivas Regal twenty-five-year-old Scotch. This is the *good* stuff, Morgan. Joyce gave it to me. I was saving it for a special occasion. Today's pretty special. Don't you think? He filled the shot glass again. I could smell the whiskey's faint aroma as he kept pouring and drinking. "This all started because of her, anyway. She said all I did was criticize her. Well, it was for her own good. She's so imperfect."

He reached into his desk drawer again, retrieving another shot glass. "Here, Morgan. Have a drink." He filled the glass and put it at the end of his desk. "Drink up," he said, waving the gun in the air, depicting merriment. I reached for the glass, even though I didn't plan on drinking. Cash kept on talking. "He wanted me to leave my wife so we could profess our love. You believe that, Morgan? He said he wanted everybody to know he loved me. What the hell was he thinking? He had a wife, too. But he didn't care about any of that, the selfish son of a ... You're not drinking Morgan." Cash said interrupting himself.

The more he spoke, the more his pain began to look like the slowly boiling rage of a narcissistic meltdown. "After all I'd done for him," he went on. "This was how he was going to treat me. I gave him so much. He wanted everybody to know we were..." He paused and miserably laughed. "He wanted everybody to know we were lovers. I couldn't let that happen." He laughed again while pouring himself another drink. " 'But Cash, you said you loved me,' " he continued, mockingly recanting his onetime lover's words as his speech began to slur. " 'You said you never wanted anything to hurt me. Well, *this* is hurting me. I don't want to be like this with you anymore. I don't want to live this lie anymore.' That selfish sissy started crying, trying to make me feel guilty. I hated it when he cried. He cried to make me feel bad. 'What's wrong with you? Stop crying! Stop it!' I told him. He wouldn't stop. So I made him stop. I hugged him until he couldn't cry anymore. I felt such relief. He stopped crying. He stopped crying."

Cash took another drink from the now almost-empty bottle of whisky, abandoning the shot glass. "Go ahead. Ask me. I know you want to know. Don't feel bad. You're just being you, Morgan. All you have to do is ask me."

I felt a hint of shame. I was no longer conflicted. I wanted to know what happened above all else. I put the shot glass of whiskey down on his desk, pulled my chair as close to the desk as I could, and looked him squarely in the eye.

"What happened the night Allister Dean lost his life?" I asked him bluntly.

Cash reached for my glass and drank the whiskey from it. I then watched his eyes grow cold and lifeless as he stared off in space and began to speak: "There. I knew I could count on you, Morgan. First things first with you, huh? This is what happened, Dr. Winters. Here ya go. I summoned him up to the bedroom and turned the music up as loud as it would go. I knew his wife was out of town. And then I begged him, one more time not to say anything about us. He refused and turned away from me. So I shot him. Then I shot him again, and then again. He lay across the tub, half-in and half-out. He looked so uncomfortable. So I pulled him out and laid him on the floor. Then I stabbed him the same way the other Audubon victims were stabbed. It was easy. He was just laying there. But I left his wedding band on his finger." A hint of sadness came across his face. He removed a knife from yet another drawer and placed it on his desk. "Then I covered him with the comforter and left. I killed him. Our secret was safe."

He lifted the bottle of whiskey into the air, as if gesturing a toast. "To Allister," he pronounced. "Here Morgan. Take these." Cash said as he turned towards a file cabinet and opened a drawer. "I won't be needing them any longer. These are the files I've been holding on to." He then raised the gun and placed the barrel into his mouth.

"Cash, NO!" I yelled.

BANG! Went the sound of the gun. Blood was everywhere.

✎ CHAPTER 14 ✎

The setting was familiar: cops everywhere, the hubbub of radio static interfering with investigative chatter, pictures being snapped in rapid succession, a corpse in the next room. Hell, I had lost count of the number of crime scenes like this I had been asked to survey over the years. But, familiar as all this was to me, this crime scene somehow didn't seem real. Everything appeared to move in blurred slow motion—almost like a dream. *Did I dream that Cash Flint, the mayor, admitted to tampering with evidence, having an affair with Allister Dean, killing him and then shooting himself in the head?* I thought. *Did that actually happen?* I shook my head, hoping for another reality. No such luck.

I was still sitting outside the mayor's office, draped in a gray blanket that shrouded the bloodstained suit I was wearing. As I slowly looked around in an attempt to recalibrate my thoughts to the here and now, I saw a silhouette of a body under a white sheet off in a distance. It was Cash.

And now you know everything.

Cash, NO! BANG! reverberated in my mind's eye as I relived the awful event. I wasn't ready to deal with the flood of emotions that come from seeing someone shoot themselves in the head. So I emotionally detached myself from the pain. I began to think instead of feel. *Where is he?* I thought as I scrutinized the crowd of police officers and officials. Slade was nowhere to be found among them.

I did, however, see another investigator swiftly walking my way. "Here we go again," I mumbled under my breath.

"I'm gonna have to ask ya some more questions, Dr. Winters," the investigator said when he approached me.

"Listen, I know the drill," I responded. "I know that's why you guys have me sitting here, but can I at least get out of these clothes? You can have 'em. I have sweats in my car. I just want out of this." I opened the blanket and gestured toward my bloodstained light gray suit.

"Sorry 'bout this, Doc, but I just need ta ask ya a couple more questions. So tell me again about the conversation you and the mayor were having."

I sighed in frustration and fatigue as I began to recount the day's events yet again.

"No, she's *not* gonna tell ya 'bout the conversation again!" went a voice behind me. I turned around in a flush of relief to see Slade standing there. He squinted as he eyed the investigator's nametag and stepped between us, then asked him, "What's your name?"

"Officer Martin Duplessis Sir."

"Well, Officer Duplessis. We're gonna let Dr. Wintahs here catch her breath, and yes, change her clothes. And we both know that you've asked her these questions enough times tonight. Her story ain't changin'. All right?"

"Yes, sir," replied the officer, and then left.

Slade turned around and handed me a pair of sweats. "Here, Wintahs, take these," he said. "I had Kendall pack some sweats for you. Let's get you out of those clothes."

"Amen," I replied as I attempted to stand, only to have my knees buckle. He caught my fall. In that moment, a flash of calm swept through my body as I held on to his rock-hard arms, re-establishing my balance. "Thank you," I whispered to him as I found myself fighting back tears.

"Yeah, I know, I know," he said reassuringly. "Come on. Let's get you out of these clothes." He put his arm around my shoulder, and we walked into one of the quartered offices. "I'll be right outside this door, Wintahs. Put your clothes in this bag. Come out when you're ready." He handed me a brown paper bag and closed the door quietly.

Despite the countless police officers and officials on the other side of the door, I couldn't remember the last time I had felt so frightened and alone. I sat for a moment in painful reflection. *He killed himself, and he murdered Allister Dean.* I took another look at my bloody suit, and suddenly an overwhelming desire to rid myself of those clothes came over me. I couldn't get undressed fast enough. I furiously unbuttoned my blouse and tore it off, along with my blazer. I unzipped my skirt while kicking off my shoes, removing everything until I was standing there in my underwear. I quickly shoved the clothes into the bag and stared at it in anger, as if I had just trapped a wild beast. "Damn you, Cash Flint," I contemptuously muttered as my knees began to grow weak again. Slade wasn't there this time, so I decided to give in to my knees, gravity, and the hurt inside. I let myself tumble onto the floor next to the bag of clothes and quietly sobbed.

After a few minutes, I heard a light knocking on the door. "You okay in theah, Wintahs?" Slade said.

"Yeah, yeah, I'm fine!" I responded, sniffing and wiping away tears. I suddenly realized I was sitting on the floor in my underwear, and I was cold. So I hurriedly put the sweats on. Once dressed, I stared at the old rustic wooden door to the office, as trepidation began to invade my thoughts: *Things will never be the same. I've just witnessed the mayor of New Orleans kill himself. Breathe, Morgan. What's that you say to your patients? The past is gone. The future is to come. Your life is now. Your thoughts are scaring you, not reality.*

I could feel a part of myself coming back. I took another deep breath and opened the door. Slade turned around and gave me the once-over. "Better?" he remarked, winked his right eye and smiled. I smiled back.

"All yours," I said as I handed him the bag of bloody clothes.

"Ya know I gotcha, huh Wintahs?" he rhetorically said, eyeing me with the concern of a trusted friend and the strength of a man. "But I need ta warn ya. There's a ton 'a' reportahs out theah, and we ain't talkin' ta none of 'em. Right?"

"Not a single one," I replied with a twinge of annoyance at the prospect of being part of a media spectacle. I allowed the irritation to fuel and distract me from everything else. *You don't have any control over any of this,* I thought, *but you do have control over how you're going to respond.* I surveyed the room again, but this time noticing the stack of victim files Cash had showed me before taking his life. They were sitting off and to the side in a chair next to the water-cooler.

"I'll take that," Slade said as he reached for the gym bag he had given me with the sweats.

"No, no, no," I replied. "I got it. I got it."

"You sure, Wintahs?"

"Yeah, I'm good. I'm going to get some water over there. I'll be right back."

"Okay, but we don't wanna hang around here much longah. They're gonna be after ya for more questions. Wanna get ya out of heah as soon as possible."

"Yeah, yeah, absolutely. Just going over there to get some water. I'll be right back, and then we can leave," I said with the tunnel vision of leaving the scene with those files. I casually walked over to the water-cooler, grabbed a cup, and dispensed some liquid as I looked around. Fortunately no one was paying any attention to me. For all they knew, I was still in the office Slade had taken me into. But I was no longer hanging around in a bloodstained suit. I was able to blend in. In one grand movement I opened the bag, placed it on the floor, and swiftly slid the files into it. I then walked back over to where Slade was standing.

"Let's get out of here," I said urgently as I took a sip of water.

"Yo!" Slade yelled, and then he whistled as his team—Leblanc, Glapion, and Anders—rushed over to where we were standing. "Detectives, it's time!"

"We gotcha covered, Doc—this is our specialty," chimed in Leblanc as the others nodded in agreement. "Besides that, Doc, I never told ya this, but I really loved your book *The Power and the Impotency of Words.* It really helped me to take a strong look at how the words I was using were either helping or hurting my wife."

"Well, ain't that sweet—Leblanc here finally learned how ta read," Glapion quipped as we all snickered in response.

"Okay, okay, you guys, knock it off, knock it off," Slade interjected. "Let's get this show on the road. You ready, Wintahs?" Slade asked as he gently looked into my eyes.

"I'm ready."

"Well, then, let's roll."

 Anders and Glapion stepped in front of me. Leblanc flanked my left, and Slade my right.

"On three," Slade commanded. "One, two, three!" He opened the door. Before them were a melée of cameras, spectators, and screaming reporters:

"Dr. Winters, did the mayor kill himself?"

"Dr. Winters, can you answer a few questions?"

"Dr. Winters, anything you want to say?"

"Dr. Winters, were you and the mayor lovers?"

Slade's team shielded me from the onslaught of endless newspeople, paparazzi, flashbulbs, microphones and onlookers. We eventually made our way to an unmarked black SUV across the street. Slade opened the backseat door. I got in and slid over. He got in next to me after surveying the surroundings one last time. Leblanc got in on the other side, Glapion called shotgun, and Anders was behind the wheel.

"Y'all okay back there?" Glapion asked from the passenger seat.

"I'm good," I quickly replied.

"Let's move," Slade ordered as we drove up St. Charles Avenue away from City Hall.

✥ CHAPTER 15 ✥

I awakened to the unfamiliar sounds of seagulls cawing and waves splashing. I stretched and yawned my way out of the old white cotton sheets and comforter that kept me warm through the night.

"You up, Wintahs?" a familiar voice from the other side of the bedroom door yelled.

"Almost," I told Slade as I quickly sat up, looking for the gym bag with the files in it. I grabbed the red-and-white plaid robe slung over a chair beside my bed, and there the bag was, on the chair. I opened it to make sure the files were still there. They were. With a sigh of relief, I put the robe on and walked out of the bedroom and into the open den and kitchen area, where Slade was standing at the stove, stirring a skillet full of sizzling bacon. I cleared my throat to flag his attention. He looked up at me and cracked his trademark crooked smile.

"Where ya at, Wintahs? Look who's up!" he said with his reassuring raspy voice. "How'd ya sleep?"

"Surprisingly well," I said, rubbing my eyes and yawning. "Is that bacon?"

"Well, I know ya don't like ta indulge too often, Wintahs, but I also know that ya love bacon. Hell, who doesn't love bacon! We keep a freezuh down heah of every kind o' bacon you could want—hickory-smoked, honey-BBQ, honey-maple, country-pepper, applewood." I giggled and put my hand over my mouth. "What? I'm just getting started. We got ya maplewood, Cajun, garlic, garlic-pepper, honey-smoked applewood, smoked maplewood."

"All right, already," I murmured to the point of tears.

"Yeah, ya right. Forrest Gump and his shrimp ain't got nothin' on me," he said, shaking his head up and down in agreement with himself as the aroma of bacon began to permeate the cabin. "Gonna be a few before everything's ready."

"You know, you didn't have to go through all this trouble, Slade."

"Trouble? *This* ain't trouble. This is my opportunity to eat some bacon. Okay?"

"Well, while you're out here with the bacon, I'm going to go take a shower."

Slade had taken me to his family's cabin in Grand Isle, an island that sits off the coast of southeastern

Louisiana in the Gulf of Mexico, about a two-hour drive from New Orleans. When we arrived the previous night, I was spent, emotionally and physically. All I remembered was Slade showing me where I would be sleeping, putting on one of his overgrown T-shirts, and collapsing on the bed. He had often talked about how nice it was up here and coming out to, as he put it, "clear his head." But his description didn't do it justice. The rustic old cabin had horizontally laid log walls and two beautiful rubble-stone fireplaces, all underneath a gable ceiling. The atmosphere was almost tranquilizing. I felt warm, comfortable and, most important, safe.

I walked into the bathroom and began to disrobe. Once completely undressed, I looked into the mirror, noticing what appeared to be a small amount of Cash's dried-up blood on my neck. Steam filled the bathroom as the mirror image grew fainter and fainter. As my reflection slowly blurred, my thoughts became clearer: *That's it, Morgan. Live in the moment, this moment.* I pulled back the shower curtain, and a rush of invitingly hot steam came pouring out. "Ahhhh," I said out loud as I stepped into the shower and reveled in the gentle sting of hot water against my naked body. "Ahhhh," I sighed again as I began to wash away the useless residue from yesterday. This shower was not only cleansing, but also rejuvenating.

Dressed in a pair of blue jeans and a form-fitting lumberjack shirt, I walked out of the bedroom and into the kitchen. The table was set with eggs, bacon, grits, orange juice, and biscuits. I was touched and impressed.

"Who knew you could cook, Slade?" I asked.

"Not too many, Wintahs—this is just a little somethin' I threw togethah," he said with a wink and a smile, while pulling out a chair for me. I smiled back, took my seat, and picked up my fork. "Wait, Wintahs. I want us to say grace. Okay?"

"Ahh, okay." We bowed our heads and put our palms together in prayer.

"God, ya know I don't do this often," Slade said solemnly. "And from what I understan', you're listenin' anyway, so I'm gonna go ahead and say some stuff out loud. So, here we go. Thank ya for this food, and thank ya for my friend being alive to tell a story. Oh, and thank ya for the bacon. Amen."

As Slade blessed the meal, I became aware that I wasn't the only one traumatized by yesterday's events. I could safely assume Slade didn't know who had been shot.

"Anything ya wanna add?" he asked me.

"As a matter of fact, there is," I said, resuming my prayer position. "I thank you for this food also, God, and for sending the person that prepared the bacon into my life. Amen."

"Yes indeed, Slade this bacon is delicious," I said as I dug in.

"Yes, it is. Don't forget the grits."

"Oh, I'm not." I reached for another piece of that succulent meat.

"Ya know, we got a lot ta take care of when we get back home. I told 'em ta give ya a day, though."

"Yeah, I know. Kind of wish we could stay out here a little longer, though. It's so peaceful." I looked around at the gradation of browns that filled the room—the medium-brown couch, the dark brown rug, the roaring fireplace.

"Yeah, been tellin' ya 'bout this place for a long time," Slade said. "This is where I go to get my mind right."

We then sat in quiet, hearing only the sounds of our forks tapping the porcelain plates, the munching of bacon, the crackling of the fireplace, and the faint caw of seagulls. I found myself waiting with bated breath and nervous tension for a right moment, but then I just decided to put my fork down and to start talking...

"Slade, Cash killed a man, covered it up, and then he shot himself," I said with relief and discomfort, as I then shook my head in consternation.

Slade glared at me. I sat up straight, putting both elbows on the table and clasped my hands together.

"I continued. "We have four dead people, and at least two killers on the loose—well, we *had* two killers on the loose. We only have *one* killer loose now. Monsignor Keegan knows about Allister Dean and the mayor. And God only knows—no pun intended—what *else* he knows."

"Back up for a minute," Slade said, putting his hand up. "Knows *what* about Allister Dean and the mayah?"

I had forgotten that Slade hadn't been inside that room with me and Cash. Nor had he been with me afterward when the investigators were questioning me. So he had the bare minimum in terms of facts.

"Brace yourself, for this one," I said.

"Considah me braced. Spill it."

"Cash was having an affair with Allister Dean for years."

"Wait—*what?*" Slade incredulously asked me in a stunned stupor.

"Yeah, for years. Dean wanted Cash to once and for all publicly profess their love and leave his wife. Cash, being the narcissist that he was, got angry at Mr. Dean for even *suggesting* going public. They argued. The next thing you know, Cash said he shot and stabbed him to make it look like the other murders. He couldn't completely replicate the other murders though. He left behind Mr. Dean's wedding ban for starters. And no skull abrasions. Then once he realized—or, rather, *thought*—that I knew all about his relationship and the cover-up, he decided he didn't want to live with the fallout. At first, his secret was worth hiding, then it was worth killing for, and ultimately he decided it was worth dying for. He evidently concluded that this truth would only set him free in death. So he shot himself in the head."

Slade looked at me in baffled curiosity. "Wait a minute," he said. "How'd you find out about Flint and Dean's relationship?"

"I wasn't positive about it, and I didn't have it all figured out, but I had a little more than a hunch," I explained. "A few days ago, Cash had stopped by my office to talk to me and see my new digs, so he said. Well, just as he arrived, one of my patients was leaving. My patient obviously knew Cash personally, and Cash obviously didn't want to acknowledge her in any way. In fact, Cash was so spooked he couldn't wait to get into my office and close the door. When we *did* get behind closed doors, he couldn't get comfortable. Anyway, I began to put the pieces together: my patient, knowing Cash; Cash being uncomfortable around said patient; Cash not even wanting to acknowledge that he knew said patient; Bryson dropping the bomb that it was Cash thwarting the investigation. I had a good hunch."

"About what?" Slade asked.

"Well I went over to his office to see what I could find out. Not having any inclination that he might have actually killed anybody, let alone Allister Dean, I asked him a few pointed questions. At first he tried to lie, then he squirmed a little. But before I knew it, he was giving me all the ugly details. He was ready to unburden himself."

I wanted to tell Slade about the files. I wanted to go through them with him, but I didn't want to risk getting him in any trouble, so I didn't.

"Don't sell ya'self short, Wintahs," Slade said. "I'm not so sure he was ready to confess. He confessed ta you." He reached for my plate. "Ya done with that?"

"Oh, yeah, you can take it."

He took the dishes into the kitchen.

"You know what, Jackson?" I asked.

"What?" Slade replied as he tilted his head to the side in curiosity.

"Let's take a break."

"A break?"

"Yeah, a break—before we have to get back to all that we're talking about. Let's soak in some of Grand Isle."

"Second best thing today."

"Dare I ask what was the first?"

"Wintahs, the bacon, the bacon," Slade replied in his usual sardonic way as we walked outside and onto the porch. We sat quietly in two old white rocking chairs, enjoying the tranquil blue-gray water of the Gulf of Mexico.

❧ CHAPTER 16 ❧

"Oh, Lawd, it's so good ta see ya, Doc. Good mornin', Doc, good mornin'. How ya' doin'?" Kendall passionately greeted me with open arms as I walked into my office for the first time since Cash killed himself. "When Commanda Slade called me and tol' me what happened, all I could think about was, 'Jesus, Mary and Joseph. What is goin' on?' "

We embraced. It was good to see her, too. After the wholeheartedly warm greeting, we went right back into doing what we usually do in the mornings before my patients start arriving. I sat in one of the waiting room chairs, Kendall sat at her desk, and we talked. But today was a little different. Kendall, who was rarely at a loss for words, was taciturn this time. I could tell she wanted to ask me about what happened, but she didn't, for some reason. So we made small talk about the weather and all the rain we had been having and how it was affecting her husband Ryder's bursitis. After those subjects had run their course, a rare but brief quiet fell upon the room, interrupted only by the sound of metal hitting porcelain as we stirred our cups of coffee. Kendall began to tap her fingernails against her cup. She couldn't stand the tense silence any longer.

"Doc, I'm not gonna ask ya' what happened, even though I wanna know," she began. "And if there's anything you wanna share in regards ta' that ill-fated afternoon, I'm all ears, okay? But I'm not gonna ask. Nope, not gonna do it. Even though I been readin' all about it in the papers and jus as sure as you're sittin' theah, I know, oh Lawd, I know theah's mo' ta' the story. But I'm not gonna ask."

Kendall's proclamation had a genuine promise, but a hope for more. She eyed me with her head cocked to the side, her eyebrows raised silently, asking me what her mouth wouldn't. *Good to be back home,* I thought with a chuckle. I walked over to refill my cup. I turned around and begin to tell Kendall about Mayor Flint's suicide, and everything else that went along with it.

"...the next thing you know, I'm back home and Slade's pulling up to my front door," I concluded.

Kendall sat back in her chair with a look of total bafflement. "I don't know where ta start, Doc," she said nervously. "Do I start with the mayuh shootin' himself? Or do I start with him tellin' you all that stuff 'bout killin' poor Mr. Dean? Or what about him throwin' all those monkey wrenches in the investigation. But wait a minute. What about that Commanda Slade savin' you from them interrogatin' ya at the 'Spanish Inquisition,' and then takin' ya to a cabin on the lake? Where do I begin? Ya know, Mother

Franklin would say that when ya don't know where ta start, 'sit down and eat yo'self an apple. It'll come to ya'. Well, I'm already sittin'. Na all I have ta do is eat an apple." Kendall then pulled a plump red apple out of her bag and bit into it.

"In other words, just sit back and relax? What you're doing isn't working? Let go and let God?" I asked her.

"Yeah, Doc. Just what I said. Sit down and eat a apple. It'll come to ya. And here it is." Kendall squinted her eyes and pursed her lips. "As strange as the mayuh was actin' the las' time he came by heah, and now we know why, there's no way I would've thought he'd killed somebody. Yeah, you always said he was hidin' somethin', but I just thought he was bein' your garden-variety sneaky politician. I liked him. Ya know?" She continued to munch on her apple.

"Yeah, I know," I responded. "I liked him, too. Cash was a very likable guy, who was also a pretty decent mayor, doing some pretty awful things though. In the end, it all became about what he could do to make the bad stuff go away—you know, fix everything but himself. In my estimation, Kendall, in his mind Cash had nothing to do with his problems. The stuff that was going wrong was always someone else's fault. His problems—or rather, his truth—became too ugly or too painful for him to acknowledge or deal with. So he created a world where all the things that went wrong, in his eyes, were someone else's fault. People do it all the time, but generally not to this extent, though. Kendall, when I was with him in that office during those last moments, I heard a man blaming the world for making him lie, cheat, and ultimately murder someone. He blamed Allister for being weak. Said he had to silence him. He blamed his wife for causing him to have an affair. He blamed me for probing him and having to tell me what happened."

I paused to take another sip of coffee as I reflected in irritation.

"You know, I'd like to think that I know how to ask a question and get an answer," I continued. "And, yeah, I usually know when I'm being lied to, but in this case, Kendall, just imagine the weight of all that stuff Cash had been carrying around trying to suppress. A secret homosexual affair that had been going on for years, killing his lover who was threatening to expose their secret, hampering the investigation of not only the man he killed, but three other murder cases. In this case, what Cash revealed wasn't so much about me being a psychiatric sleuth, as it was about a man desperately wanting out of the prison of lies he'd placed himself in."

I took another sip of coffee and looked at the black-and-white print hanging on the wall. Upon first glance it appeared to depict people climbing stairs in a multi-storied dwelling. But, as you look closer, you see that some of the stair wells lead to nowhere or another one might be on the wall or on the ceiling. The print is called 'Relativity' by M.C. Escher, who was famous for creating optical illusions in his artistry. His prints were never what they seemed upon first glance—just like Cash, these murders, and most things in life. I hung it on the wall to remind my patients to always dig deeper. That's where freedom is: beyond the surface.

Kendall exasperatingly sighed. "Yes, indeed," she said. "I do remember you saying, though, that he had a side to his personality that he wasn't showin' everybody."

"Yeah, I did say that. And my next thought would always be, so do many politicians. So do many people. But with Cash, I did see him growing more and more manipulative and self-serving while attempting to remain the baby-kissing, handshaking, smiling politician for the public."

"Whatcha think happened to him?"

"I think that over time his magnetic gift of a personality ultimately became fused with the chest-beating, immediately gratifying coping mechanism of narcissism, which is often a result of not dealing with hurts from the past. He had to have been coping this way for a long time to have done the things he did. After a certain point, it's hard to get a person to rethink how and why they do things, even if they're figuratively and literally killing the people around them. He was concentrating on preserving the veneer that he'd created, saving face—the face he'd charmed and beguiled people with most of his life, I presume. As long as what they want the public to see remains intact, they see themselves as winning, until—"

"Until the wall comes crashin' down, huh Doc, until the cows come home, until the fat lady starts singin'. And guess what, Doc? The walls came down. All the cows came home, and the fattest lady I know started singin' like a bird."

I chuckled at Kendall's exclamation point, as I went on to say, "the truth is that Cash chose to suppress evidence, Allister Dean, the truth, and his feelings and take matters into his own hands. Life just doesn't work that way. People mistakenly tell themselves, 'I don't have to feel this. I'll just suck it up, and it'll go away.' "

"But when you suck it up, it's gonna come out somewhere. Right, Doc?"

"You got it. And in Cash's case, it perversely came out in the form of adultery, murder, obstruction of justice, and suicide. Narcissism is a terrible way of not dealing with trauma or pain. In fact, not dealing with pain or loss is a terrible way of being. It's a choice of a slow death."

"It's what you always say about stuffin' emotions, detachin', tryin' to control instead of feelin' huh Doc?"

"Yep. When you get down to it, we know that there's no escaping our uncomfortable hurt-filled feelings."

Kendall sighed again. "Wow, I tell ya, Doc, if I didn't know before, I sure know now about all the bad stuff that comes from suppressin' and repressin'. Oh, Lawd, don't do it! Surrender, give in, feel it, whatever it is. Feelin' that feelin' might hurt, but it ain't gonna kill ya', but, not feelin' sure could, and in the mayor's case it killed him and somebody else. Ya know, I think that's what Mother Franklin meant when she talked about

God not givin' ya any mo' than you can carry. People not trustin' that He's gonna be there for the hurt and the tears. I s'pose they think that the pain and tears are just gonna turn 'em ta dust or something, huh?"

We both sat there for a moment, gazing off into nowhere, when Kendall broke the silence. "I just remembered that ya tol' me that that fine Commanda Slade took ya out to his cabin for two days. I think ya might actually be thinkin' I'm not gonna ask ya 'bout that. Well, I didn't ask ya 'bout the mayor. You volunteered that information." She impishly smiled. "But sure as I tell ya, I'm gonna ask 'bout Commanda Slade and that cabin. You bes' believe that. Now what happened at the cabin, Doc?"

Before I could answer, the phone rang. "Oh, shoot," Kendall said as she picked up.

"No comment. Thank you very much and now you have a nice day. One of those pesky reporters, okay, Doc," she eagerly continued as she put the phone down. "You were just getting ready to tell me about Commanda Slade takin' you out to the romantic cabin."

I love it, I thought. *Leave it to Kendall to take away some of the sting by asking about Slade and the cabin.*

"Well, if you really want to know," I responded.

"You know I do, Doc," Kendall chimed in excitedly.

"He was just the person you think he would be under those circumstances."

"And who is it that?" Kendall asked, wanting all the details I was willing to give. Her playful inquisition was an enjoyable distraction.

"He was strong, deliberate, intense, kind, nurturing. Need I go on?"

"Please do." Kendall released a joyous smile.

"He wanted to take care of me. I let him, for a change. You know how you're always telling me that I should relax? Well, I did." I said as I glanced at the small TV screen in the reception area. "Wait a minute. Turn that up."

"What?"

"The TV. Turn it up. That's Haddock at City Hall in front a bevy of microphones."

Kendall turned up the volume. "Dr. Winters hasn't been out there fighting crime," Dr. Haddock was saying on the screen. "The fine women and men in blue, along with the good citizens of New Orleans and their tips, are the real heroes, not Dr. Winters. As the Coroner, I thank her for wanting to help, but I think it's time we put Dr. Morgan Winters and her contributions—or not—into perspective. There's nothing extraordinary about what she does. She's a fine psychiatrist, and I'm not saying that she hurt any of the cases she's worked on, as far as I know. But clearly, as you can see with the mayor, sometimes she goes too far."

"Has Dr. Winters harmed any of the investigations she's been asked to help with Dr. Haddock?" asked a news reporter.

"Dr. Haddock, are you saying that Dr. Winters had something to do with the mayor's death?" asked another.

"I can't answer that," replied the coroner. "But what I will say is that I believe she's way too involved in police business." Haddock then stepped away from the cluster of microphones.

"That was New Orleans Coroner Dr. William Haddock commenting on the tragic event that took place here at City Hall just a few days ago," said the news reporter. "He described Dr. Winters as being helpful at times, but was highly critical of what he described as her 'over-involvement in police business.' He also fell short of stating that she had something to do with the death of Mayor Flint. This, of course, comes on the heels of the suicide death of the Mayor here at City Hall in the presence of Dr. Winters. If you'll recall, Dr. Winters was first made known to us as the testifying expert in the murder trial of Boudreaux Dupré, 'The Beignet King.' I think we have some footage."

An archival interview with me about my testimony in Dupré's trial appeared on the screen: "Dr. Winters, it sounds like you've already concluded that Boudreaux Dupré is not a liar and that he did not plot, plan, connive, maliciously murder his wife, and then create this smokescreen of false alibis?"

"No," I said, "what I'm telling you is that, in order for Mr. Dupré to have committed this crime, his profile, the thing that I'm here to give my expert opinion on would dictate psychological, sociological, factual, and interpretative inconsistencies with what we know about him and his late wife. You didn't call me up here to present you with an alibi or physical evidence to convict Mr. Dupré. You called me up here on this stand to give you my professional opinion. I've done that for the last—um—I'd say hour and a half." At that point I was annoyingly looking at my watch. "Your verbal gymnastics are not going to change my conclusions, or my testimony. My expert opinion says that this man is innocent. If you want to hear otherwise, call someone one else to the stand."

"Boy, that was some trial, huh, Clark?" the reporter asked the main news anchor.

"It sure was," Clark responded.

"Well, what we know about Dr. Winters since then is that she's been somewhat of a local psychiatric sleuth. She's been given credit for having helped the NOPD solve about fifteen murder cases. They say she has the uncanny ability to get people to reveal things. The question is, what all did the mayor reveal to Dr. Winters before he took his life? My sources tell me, Clark, that Dr. Winters went to see the mayor the day he took his life to talk to him about what she believed to be serial murder-type killings that were going uninvestigated. I was also told that Mayor Flint was being implicated in the death of Grammy Award-winning artist Allister Dean, who as we know was found shot and stabbed to death in his uptown Audubon Place home. We're not quite certain what to make out of all of this. But as we know more, we'll pass it on to you. We reached out to Dr. Winters, but she has not yet returned any of our calls for comment. That's all for now. This is Karen Broussard reporting live from City Hall. Back to you, Nancy."

Kendall muted the volume of the set and turned my way. "That Dr. Haddock is something else, ain't he, Doc?"

"Yeah he's a piece of work, but I can't worry about him right now."

"Well, I don't like him. I don't think I ever did. And you know I love everybody, Doc. But I found it hard to even like him..."

As Kendall continued, a tinge of discomfort ran through my body, believing that in this case Haddock might have been right. I had actually taken files from a crime scene. *Who do you think you are*? I thought. *You couldn't trust that they were going to do anything with the files. They'd been hiding all kinds of information, and look what happened*, I told myself, attempting to justify my actions. But, in reality, I knew better. I knew I had a bit of a control issue that could rear its ugly head whenever I became unnerved. And I was certainly unnerved after Cash shot himself in the head. Instead of feeling all of that bad stuff that goes along with watching someone kill himself, I became angry and decided that I needed to take over the investigation. *Who do you think you are?* I asked myself in condemnation. But then, quickly rushing to my own defense, *You're Dr. Morgan Jane Winters, a human being that gives a damn, and you're gonna figure this one out.*

"...Ya know what I'm saying Doc?" Kendall went on. "He is not to be trusted."

"Yes I do," I said. "Kendall, look at the time. I've got to look over these charts before the patients start arriving."

"Well, before you get started Doc, I jus wanna say, I'm glad you're back."

"I am, too, Kendall." I smiled affectionately at her and then made my way into my office.

I put my briefcase down and sat in the chair behind my desk. I sighed, feeling a sense of further comfort in the normalcy of Kendall, my office, and my desk. I grabbed today's patient-load of files as I glanced at my bag, where the files from Cash's office still lingered.

Look at 'em, I thought. *Just take a peek, Morgan.*

As much as I enjoyed reading police reports, I hadn't taken a look at these yet. "Just do it!" I chided myself as I reached for the manila folders sitting just inside my bag next to the files Slade had given me.

I opened that first folder to one of Haddock's preliminary autopsy reports. As I began to read it, I was taken by the amount of detail included, but more so by the amount of detail *not* included in the reports Haddock had given me.

Wait a minute, I thought. *These autopsy notes look completely different from the ones Haddock gave me. They're both listed as preliminary and dated around the same time. The differences are extreme. Thirteen stab wounds, thirteen stab wounds, thirteen stab wounds. What's going on? Was Haddock part of the cover up? Why would he falsify evidence though?* Just then the phone rang, quickening my thought to the sound of the phone.

"Doc, it's Dr. Sanchez." Kendall announced through the intercom.

"Oh, great. I have something I would love to run by her."

"Dr. Winters will be with you in a moment," Kendall said into the phone.

I picked up the phone. "Carla. Hey."

"Hey yourself," said the voice from the other end. "I've been seeing you all over the news. I've been trying to call you. How are you, my friend?

"I'm fine. Sorry about the disappearing act. My phone and I were on lockdown for a couple of days. Trying to let some of this blow over."

"So everything I've been seeing on the news is true. You were there when the mayor—"

"Yes, I was," I said abruptly. "Words can't describe how awful it was."

"I can only imagine, *mi amiga.* Well, what can I do for you? Is there anything I can do?"

"As a matter of fact, there is."

"You name it."

"I know this is last minute, but are you available for lunch today? I have something I want to run by you. I'll come to you, Carla."

"Let's see. Hold on a sec, and let me check my calendar. Yeah, I just had a meeting cancellation. We're in luck. We can do lunch. We can eat at the café in the building."

"Okay, see you at noon." I handed the phone back to Kendall.

❧ CHAPTER 17 ❧

"My friend, from what I know of the autopsy report process, both preliminary and final, it would be impossible for these two to be so different and for the same person," Carla asked me as she scrutinized the pages of the respective autopsy reports from Cash's and Haddock's offices. "Did Haddock give these to you?"

"Yeah, he put them in my hand," I replied.

"You're kidding me. That low-life."

"It's okay. I'm going to take care of this today."

"What are you going to do?"

"Gonna deal with it head on," I replied with the cold stare of disdain for Haddock's actions.

"Oh, boy," Carla said. "If Haddock had any clue, he'd be afraid of you right about now."

"And I know I don't have to say this to you, but this is strictly between—"

"I know. I know, *mi amiga.* Mum's the word. But, what a low-life. He's gonna get his one day."

"Maybe sooner than later."

"Go get 'em, girl."

*   *   *   *

"Hi, Maslow," I said to my dog as he pranced, jumped up and down and wagged his tail, happy to see me. "That's right. Mommie's home. Mommie's home." I quickly put my keys on my kitchen counter and my briefcase on the floor before I playfully rubbed Maslow's belly and scratched behind his ears. After a moment of escape through Maslow's blissful joy, I happily kicked off my four-inch heels while shuffling through the mail. "Electricity bill, water bill, cable bill, QVC bill. Same-ol'-same-ol', Maslow," I said out loud as I placed the mail on the counter, mindlessly grabbed the remote control and thumbed the power on.

"Nancy, our sources tell us that the mayor was leading a double life..." *Click* went the TV as I consciously switched it off. I had heard enough of that conversation in my own head. And I certainly didn't want to hear the media's endless spin on what happened.

"You know what," I told Maslow, "tonight's the night. I'm going to open it." I reached in my cooler for a bottle of wine I had been saving for some unknown special occasion. *I'm clear now,* I thought. *Every day I'm alive is special.* I eyed the label on the bottle. *Castle Rock-Cabernet Sauvignon, 2009—this is going to be nice.* I popped the cork and poured myself a glass as I made my way into the den. I put the bottle and my glass on the coffee table in front of the fireplace.

It was a cool night, and my beautiful old home could be drafty at times, but there was something uniquely different about cold nights in New Orleans. At times it could be damp and heavy, with the frigid air going through your clothes and skin until it reached your bones and other days it could be as warm as summer. I grabbed a log, put it in the fireplace, lit a few matches and tossed them in. I stood there until the flame slowly sizzled and cracked its way to a low brilliance. "Perfect!" I said out loud, holding my hands over the fireplace as the heat began to slowly permeate the room.

I took another sip of my Castle Rock. "Yes indeed," I said. "What a day, Maslow. Hell, what a week. Cash taking his life. Haddock taking an opportunity to throw me under the bus." My terrier snuggled up next to me on the sofa. I sipped some more, reached for my gym bag, and pulled out the stack of files Cash had held onto.

As the night went on I read and reread the heap of information, only to conclude that the only reason Cash was sitting on these files was to hide the inconsistencies of Allister Dean's murder from the other three. The other victims' reports read almost identically, with no massive amount of evidence to be uncovered about the other three murders.

Look at this, I thought. *Finally, full-bodied pictures, including hands. And just as I suspected, the only one wearing a ring is Allister Dean, meaning that the killer probably has three wedding rings or bands in his possession. Ah, yes.*

I sifted through the preliminary autopsy reports. *This is just confirming what we already know. Whoever killed these three people was right-handed according to the angles of the stab wounds and these notes. Dean's angles were that of a lefty, like Cash.*

I continued to turn pages. The more I read through the files, the more questions I had. But one thing was for sure, though—they all worshipped at Sacred Heart Cathedral. My gut was telling me to narrow my focus.

He's right here in our midst. But you don't want to force an outcome. That's the best way to get at what I want to believe happened, but not necessarily the truth. Stay focused, Morgan. You want the truth, and the truth is not created. It just is.

What's this last entry? Do they all have this entry? I quickly turned the pages. '*semi-precious stone found next to the body, semi-precious stone found next to the body, semi-precious stone found next to the body.' Am I seeing things? You know what? I'm gonna pick this back up tomorrow.* I yawned and peered down at my dog, who was struggling to keep his eyes open with me.

Suddenly, the doorbell rang. Maslow's head lifted in alertness. "Who could that be?" I asked him as I made my way to the front door. I looked through the peephole, and all I could see was a red-haired older man in a gray-and-brown uniform holding his head down. I couldn't really see his face. "Who is it?" I yelled.

"Special delivery for Dr. Winters," went the voice.

Funny, I wasn't expecting anything and it was kind of late, I thought as I removed the chain and opened the door, The man lifted his head to present a familiar but disingenuous smile.

"Don't I know you?" I asked, immediately recognizing him as the security guard from the coroner's office building.

"Yes you do, Doctor, and I have something for you—" I noticed that he didn't have a package. I grew suspicious.

"How did you get my address? You know what? I'll pick up whatever you have for me from your station." I closed and locked the door. Irritated fear swept through my body as he began to shake the door handle. "I'm calling the police!" I yelled as I dialed 911.

"What is the nature of the emergency?" asked the 911 operator.

"You don't have to do that, Doctor!" went the man's voice in irritated desperation. "I just want to give you something. Open the door, Doctor!" He jiggled the handle.

"I have a man trespassing on my property, and I feel threatened," I told the operator over the phone.

"What is your location?" she asked as I gave her the information while looking through the peephole. I could see the man swiftly walking away. No sooner than two minutes later, a siren could be heard coming down the road.

*   *   *   *

"...And you're sure that's who he is?" the police officer asked me as we wrapped up their visit.

"Positive," I said firmly. "Just like I said. He's the security guard from the Jefferson building, and his last name is Jones."

"Okay, then. This should be easy. We'll give you a call as soon as we find him, Doctor. Oh, also, we got an order to leave a squad car in front the house.

"What?"

"Yeah, at least for tonight. This is Officer Smith. Okay?"

"Nice to meet you, Officer Smith, but I don't think all of this is necessary."

"Not up for debate, Doctor. This came from the boss." I squinted my eyes and furrowed my brow in confusion.

"Superintendent Bryson. So car's gonna be parked right there."

Just then my phone rang. It was Slade. "Hold on one minute, Officer," I said. "Slade, hey."

"You all right?" he asked from the other end.

"I'm fine. How'd you find out so quickly?"

"Never mind that. You okay, right?"

"Yeah. I'm fine. Officers Smith and Triggs are here doing their job. In fact, a detail's been ordered to sit out in front of my house tonight. You know anything about that?"

"I might have called a certain superintendent and requested such. But I ain't tellin'."

"You didn't have to do that."

"I know that, Wintahs. Sometimes I just do what I wanna do. Okay?"

"Well, do you want to meet me for breakfast tomorrow? I want to run some ideas by you. Dookie Chase for nine?"

"See you then."

*   *   *   *

The next day at Dookie Chase's, Slade took a drink from his glass of water and wiped his mouth with the white cloth napkin from his lap. He folded his arms, placed them on the table, leaned toward me, looked up, and raised his left eyebrow and the left corner of his mouth.

"So," he said, and paused for a moment. "How ya doin', Wintahs? And before you answer, don't give me all that mumbo-jumbo 'bout 'I'm fine.' This is what *I* do. You're talkin' ta *me.*" He then leaned in a little closer and lowered his raspy voice even more. "How ya doin'?" he asked again as I was distracted by how attractive his protective inquiry was. His deep-set brown eyes were speaking volumes. He even smelled good. I blinked my eyes a couple of times, attempting to flip the mental switch back to the here-and-now. He sat there, looking at me, waiting for an answer.

I gathered my thoughts and ventured a response: "The truth is, I *am* fine, Slade."

He took a deep, almost disapproving breath.

"No, now, wait a minute," I said as I put my hand on top of his big, rugged hand. "When I say that I'm fine, I don't mean that I'm happy all the time or that I don't have moments that bring me to tears thinking about what happened or that I've worked through all of this. I'm taking it as it comes. Sometimes I'm doing it right. Sometimes I'm not." I flashed back to seeing myself take those files from City Hall the day Cash took his life. "I tell my patients to deal with it, or it'll deal with you. Well, I'm trying to deal with it. I'm not running from it—progress, Slade, not perfection. So, I am fine, and yes, this is what I do," I concluded with a smirk and a wink.

"Okay," said Slade. "Can't argue with that." He resumed eating his eggs and grits.

"Thank you for caring, though, and thank you for Officer Smith last night," I told him.

"Whatever, Wintahs. That's what I do." He winked and smiled in return. "Oh, by the way, you know, the darndest thing—some files went missin' from City Hall pertainin' ta the murdah cases the night Cash took his life. You know anythin' 'bout that, Wintahs?"

"Ahh, no," I replied in a pathetic attempt to lie to Slade. But he could see right through me.

"Aw, come on, Wintahs."

"What?"

"Whateva, Wintahs. Just make it work." Slade shook his head and rolled his eyes.

"We done with that conversation?" I asked as Slade just looked at me with his mouth twisted to the side.

"Okay, good," I replied to my own question, wanting to move on. "Slade, my gut is telling me stronger than ever now that we find a deeper connection to Sacred Heart other than attendance—we find the murderer."

"Still on the Sacred Heart trail, huh?"

"Even more so. No, I don't have anything new, but there's something there. I can just feel it. I'm going over there later this afternoon. Are you free?"

"Think so."

"Good. But before I do that, though, I'm going to give Haddock a visit. I have a few questions for him."

Slade chuckled as his phone began to ring. "I knew it," he said, frustrated. "This might put a monkey wrench in us meetin' at Sacred Heart." He checked the caller ID and picked up. "Slade here... Yes, sir... Yes... Okay... Half an hour? Yes sir... Right away." He ended the call and tucked away his phone. "Well, so much for us meetin' at Sacred Heart this evening," he told me. "That was the chief. I gotta go in ASAP, and it's gonna be a while before I'm free. I might be able to meet up with you later, but I don't know for sure. No point in me asking you to wait, is there?"

"Nope," I said as I finished my last sip of coffee.

"I'll call you later. I gotta run, Wintahs. Be careful"

❧ CHAPTER 18 ❧

"What is this pile of misinformation?" I said exasperatedly as I plopped the short stack of autopsy reports onto Haddock's desk. His mouth dropped open, and his eyes grew wide in surprise.

"What the hell is this, Winters?" he said, shocked. *There it was, as if I needed it*, I thought. His expression of stupefaction lingered way too long for it to be real. He knew exactly what I was talking about the minute he saw the reports. His plea of ignorance was a lie.

"How did you get in here?" he threatened. "I'm calling security."

"Oh, we both know that you're not going to call security," I countered. "Better yet, you want *me* to call 'em? When I call um, me, security, the police chief, and the superintendent can all have a nice little talk."

Haddock just sat there, staring at me with the same mien of feigned shock and outrage.

"Yeah, I didn't think so," I said. "So instead of me *or* you calling security, you can just tell me why you gave me fictitious autopsy reports."

Haddock's eyes darted about the room. "I don't know what the hell you're talking about," he said defensively. "I didn't give you any fictitious reports." He scratched his nose and sniffed in discomfort. "You got the same thing everybody else got." He was practically giving a clinic on what liars do when they're lying. He stood up and began to raise his voice. "How dare you come in here and impugn my integrity. I'll have your license for this, Winters. This is an egregious display of unprofessionalism. You know, it's people like you, Winters," he said with exaggerated disdain. "It's people like you that disrupt the flow and cause bad things to happen. It wasn't a coincidence that the mayor died in your presence."

It was clear he was attempting to intimidate me and throw a smokescreen. He was attempting to shift the conversation to me, hoping that I would feel the need to defend myself from either his behavior or his hateful accusations regarding the mayor. But that ship sailed a long time ago. *I'm not one of his employees,* I thought. *I'm not that easily distracted, and he doesn't scare me.* I knew he was lying. And by now, he knew I knew he was lying. I walked over to his desk and got as close to him as my own comfort would allow. I then looked him dead straight in his eyes, and with a steely-edged tone above a whisper I began to express to Dr. Haddock the truth as I saw it.

"You listen to me, Haddock," I told him straight out. "You're lying, which makes you a liar. That's right. You're a *liar!* So if you think that all this drama is going to change what I know to be true, think again. What I just put on your desk are two copies of two different reports for the same person, for the same date, and they both have your seal of approval. So the only thing I really want to hear from you right now is *why.* And don't even think about trying to blame this on anybody else. I know that these reports go through you, and nobody else. So I'm asking you one more time. Why are there two versions of this report?"

He folded his arms. His breathing was heavy, and his brows were furrowed. I could tell he was uncomfortably angry, not being used to people challenging or questioning him, especially a woman. But that was precisely how to knock him off of his ugly game. He was nothing but a bully, and bullies usually back down when they're confronted. We stood, deadlocked in unnerving silence.

Haddock finally sat down in his chair, still looking like he had some fight in him. But then a glare of sadness and bewilderment appeared to set in as I stood there, waiting for him to speak. He began to chuckle. "You got me, you got me," he said. "The reports are different, Winters. Because I doctored them. I've *been* doctoring the reports I give to you. And if the mayor wouldn't have killed himself, you would have never known." He shamelessly looked up at me with a sinister smile.

"To what end?" I pressed. "Why?"

"Why do you think Winters? To stop you. To slow down the damn crime-fighting machine of Dr. Winters." He turned down the sides of his mouth in disdain. "I don't like you. I don't know if I ever did. I got so sick and tired of you coming to every crime scene as if you were God's gift to the city of New Orleans. 'Let her in,' " he mimicked. " 'Is Dr. Winters here yet?' 'We can't start the investigation until Dr. Winters gets here.' Don't touch anything until she gets here. Who the hell are you?" He lifted his head in contemptuous anger as he pursed his already thin lips. "I've been the coroner here for the last twenty five years," he continued furiously. *"Twenty-five years! Where's my respect? Where's my damn red carpet?"* He let out another anguished chuckle. "So, with great pleasure, I painstakingly omitted phrases, sentences, words, whatever I could, to make your work a little harder. At first I was just leaving out a phrase or two. But as time went on I left out more and more. Then, I started adding things. The changes got bigger and bigger. It felt good. Every time I handed you a report I got a rush. But, no matter what I did, you always found a way to get the bad guy. And here we are again. You catching the bad guy. But this time, I guess the bad guy is me, huh?"

"Where do you get off playing God in such a selfish, destructive way?" I interrupted. "You dislike me so much that you're willing to let murderers roam the streets?"

"Nobody else got doctored reports, Winters—just you. Besides, you always caught um anyway. Didn't you?"

He replied and cynically laughed as he looked up at me.

At this point, I actually felt sorry for Haddock. He was naked, his insecurities blindingly vivid. He just sat there, staring off into a distance out of the cloudy office window behind his desk—a far cry from his usual bombastically pompous disposition. "You don't have to worry about me in this job any longer, Winters. I'm done." As Haddock lamented those words, my heart began to race as I flashed back to Cash's confession and demise. *Oh, God, not again,* I thought.

"I'm out of here. I give up," Haddock said as he opened a manila folder sitting on his desk. He then held up the lone piece of paper in the folder for me to see. It was a letter of retirement and resignation. "Here, take these." He reached into his desk drawer and dropped a stack of pictures on top of his desk.

"What's this?" I asked looking down at them.

"I'm leaving. You stay as long as you want." He picked up his briefcase and jacket and walked out the door. My sense of calm was restored. *And there it is again— the truth setting someone else free,* I thought as I looked through the stack of pictures.

↜ CHAPTER 19 ↝

I had been sitting in Sacred Heart's parking lot for a while now. The sun was beginning to set. *Hmmm. They all look the same*, I thought as I went through the stack of pictures Haddock had left. *Except this one.* I held it up to extract a better view. *What's that?* I wondered as I looked at what appeared to be a rather large garnet stone lying next to Ronan Tate's head. I flipped back through the pictures and noticed similar stones next to Victoria Gaines' and Paige Brook's heads as well.

Just then, my phone began to ring, startling me out of my deep concentration. I quickly grabbed it. It was Slade.

"Let me guess. You're on your way?" I wishfully said.

"No such luck, Wintahs. Just as I thought. I'm stuck here at the precinct for a while. Ya been ta see Haddock yet?"

"Yep."

"Find out anything?"

"Yep."

"Whatcha got?"

"He's resigning."

"What?"

"You heard me. He's resigning."

"What the heck?"

"Yeah, I know. Doesn't change the rest of my mission for today, though."

With the phone pressed between my ear and my shoulder I removed the key from the ignition and stuffed the photos into my purse. I then got out of the car and began to walk through the parking lot toward the church entrance.

"I'd like ta tell ya that I'll be there in a li'l while, but I can't," Slade continued. "We've got a butt-load of paperwork ta go through surrounding the mayuh's death that Bryson wants done now. So I don't know how long I'm gonna be. But as soon as I'm done, I'm headed over."

"Okay. Sounds good."

"You be careful. Don't take any chances. Ya see anything bad, get outta theah. Things are different now. Ya know what I mean?"

"I know what you mean. And you know I'll get out if there's any danger."

"No, I don't know that. But do it today." We both chuckled.

I made it up the cathedral's large concrete stairs and pulled open one of its big, heavy double doors. I stepped in and looked around, taking in the familiar reverent silence. Something felt different—I wasn't sure if it was me or the church, though. Cash's suicide was still haunting me. So, for certain, my senses were on high alert.

I walked up the middle isle of the storied house of God. The smell of prayer candles burning, the echoing sound of my heels against the marble floors, and the sound of the AC kicking on and off were more pronounced than usual. *Hmmm, the confessionals*, I thought as I continued to walk and look for anything that would lend itself to a clue.

I noticed the mahogany confessional built into the wall of the church, where it stood tall and regal with intricately carved crucifixes and likenesses of Jesus. Each one maintained three separate compartments; the smaller compartments, for the penitents, the confessors, the sinners, sat on both sides of the larger middle section, which was where the priest sat. I took a quick glance around the church to make sure I was alone. I then made the sign of the cross. "Forgive me, father," I avowed out loud in a whisper, then opened the door of the middle section of the confessional and walked in.

My eyes grew as wide as quarters as I took in the visuals of the sanctum. It was smaller than I had imagined—nothing ornate or august, as the main sanctuary and my imagination might have suggested. It was a modest, ligneous room. The dark wooden bench where the priest sat was worn, discolored, and smooth to the touch. I sat down on it. I then looked to my right and my left to see the dark gray mesh screens placed over for what, to many, would be a window to someone's soul. The screens divided, opened, and hid the person or penitent on the other side as he or she knelt and confessed sins. I slid the thin wooden panel covering the screen back and forth, attempting to capture the full experience, but I couldn't. The other side of the screen was dark and lifeless. I then ran my hand along the wall that supported the bench I was sitting on, noticing something odd about it. It didn't look like the rest of the wood in the confessional. It was slightly lighter in color, and more hollow and thin.

As I began to observe the wall more closely, a familiarly deep, resonant voice from outside the confessional made itself known: "Can I help you?"

"Uh-oh," I whispered as I stepped out of the confessional and into the nave of the church to see Monsignor Keegan staring back at me.

"Monsignor!" I responded as the tall clergyman stood before me, eyeing me in unabashed repudiation. "Ahhh, I didn't see you there. Where'd you come from?"

"Well, how could you see me, Dr. Winters? You were in the oratory."

"Yes, I was," I confidently replied, hoping we could simply ignore that reality. No such luck, though. He continued on.

"I saw you when you came in the front door. And then I surprisingly watched you go into the confessional."

"You saw me come in?"

"Yes. You seemed to be quite captivated in thought. And now I know why. Evidently you had a confession to hear."

"Okay, Monsignor. My heartfelt apologies for the invasion of church code," I offered as I was momentarily brought back to the sixth grade and Father Davellier chastising me for peeping into the priest's compartment of the confessional. I was given quite the lecture and a detention for that.

Wait a minute, I thought. *You're not twelve, and he's not Father Davellier. You've apologized. Move on, Morgan. Besides, you got in this time.* I thought and internally smiled.

Coming back to my adult self in the here and now, I said, "Monsignor, I'm here because I strongly believe that when we figure out all the reasons how and why Victoria Gaines, Ronan Tate and Paige Brook's murders are tied to Sacred Heart, we'll figure out who killed them."

"Is that so?"

"Yes," I responded without missing a beat—or rather, before he could take a breath. "Monsignor, tell me, how did you know them?" His demeanor quickly went from displeasure to discomfort. I caught him off guard. He nervously cleared his throat.

"Well, Dr. Winters, they were all a part of the Sacred Heart family, just like you, except they attended Mass a bit more regularly." He rounded the corner of his mouth in a bemused smile.

I smiled back, as I was reminded of how hard it was to keep Msgr. Keegan off guard. He could be thrown a little off balance for a moment, but then he got right back on his feet. I just kept plowing away, though—I thought it and asked it, no matter how seemingly invasive it was.

"Monsignor," I began, "I know more than anyone the importance of confidentiality, but did they divulge anything earth-shattering in confession?"

He continued to maintain his stoic posture, but this time clenched his jaw in irritation. "Dr. Winters, I'm going answer you by quoting the Code of Canon Law, specifically 983.1."

Oh, Lord, I thought. *I asked for it.*

" 'It is a crime for a confessor in any way to betray a penitent by word or in any other manner or for any reason,'" he recited. "So, Dr. Winters, it is with this code from the Catechism that I respectfully decline to answer your question as to what any of the victims might have revealed, God rest their souls, in confession."

"Oh, I understand, Monsignor. I just have such a strong desire to see their murderer or murderers brought to justice. You know what I mean?" I gave myself a moment to process the fact that the Monsignor had just unwittingly told me he had actually seen them in confession.

I then showed him the pictures Haddock had just given me. "Anything look familiar here?" I asked the Monsignor, once again looking for a shock value payoff and hoping to knock him off his game. His raised eyebrows and rounded eyes initially suggested surprise at what he was looking at, but his expression quickly turned into one of someone seeing something familiar. He held one of the pictures closer, then further away, turned it sideways, and squinted.

"You see something you recognize, Monsignor?"

"The stones next to their skulls look like the ones from the church chalice—*my* chalice," he said, and then slowly began to walk toward the altar. I followed him. We entered the red-carpeted, white-walled sacristy, where vestments and other church valuables were kept. My eyes were immediately fixated on the brilliant purple robes carefully laid out on the creden, a waist-high, dresser-like wooden structure with very slender drawers. He didn't walk toward the robes, but toward a rather nondescript light brown cabinet above the sink on the other side of the room. He reached into his pocket and pulled out a key that was attached to a sterling silver key-ring resembling a small rosary. He opened the cabinet, where a large, heavily engraved sterling cup sat on a red velvet-like material. It was the chalice for Sacred Heart. He reached for the cup. "See," he said. "They are distinctively representative of my family and Sacred Heart. They are very unique." He pointed to the engravings and the stones on the chalice. "It was given to me by my family when I was ordained."

I leaned in to get a better look. "Yes it does, Monsignor," I said in amazement. "Who else has access to this cabinet and/or the sacristy?"

"Only myself and Father John. And he's been on sabbatical for a year. Wait a minute." He paused for a moment. "We keep a spare key under here." He walked back toward the creden, reached into the bottom drawer and under one of the vestments. Then he pulled the vestment completely back. "Where is it?" he questioned as he opened and closed the rest of the drawers. "It's been in here for years."

"A spare key?" I asked.

"Yes! It's gone!"

"How long have you been keeping the chalice under lock and key, Monsignor? And why?"

"Well, Doctor, as we announced some time ago, the church was burglarized earlier this year. Since then, we've kept the chalice under lock and key."

"But you still leave the front doors unlocked."

"Yes. This is God's house. These doors will always be open."

"Okay. Who else might know about that key and have access, Monsignor?"

"Like I said, Doctor," he replied, this time with hint of familiar irritation in his voice, "other than myself and Father John, no one."

"No one?"

"No one."

"No one?" I asked one more time.

"Doctor, how many times must I say this to you? *No one else*—well..." He stifled his answer in contemplation.

"Well, what?"

"Well, there is Mr. Grimes, the church custodian. He has access to everything, and it's highly likely that he knew about the extra key."

"Really? Does Mr. Grimes have an office or an area that he works out of?"

"Of course." Msgr. Keegan placed the chalice back into the cabinet, locked it up, and put the key back into his pocket. Then, without uttering a word, he walked out of the sacristy and back to the nave of the church toward the confessionals as I followed him. We stopped at an old brown door on the same wall the confessionals sat on, but just a little further down. "This is Mr. Grimes' office," he said. "It's considered his custodial space."

"Do you think he's in there?" I asked as we stood there in front of the door.

"He's usually gone home by now, but if he's not, he could be anywhere on the grounds, Doctor." Monsignor replied as we continued to hold court in place.

"Okay, then, there's only one way to find out for sure," I responded as I reached around the Monsignor and knocked on the door. No response. I knocked again. Without saying a word, he reached into his pants pocket to pull out yet another set of keys. Placing it into the keyhole he slowly turned the key to the left, then quickly to the right, eliciting the clicking sounds of a door being unlocked. He then slowly began to turn the doorknob. The door squeaked as he slowly opened it.

"Mr. Grimes," Monsignor called out as we stood in slight trepidation, waiting for a reply. There was none. So we cautiously began to walk into the unlit room. The air was stagnant and filled with the smell of cleaning products and old wood. A string hung from the ceiling for the light. I pulled on it with no success. I pulled again and again until finally it came on.

"Whewww, let there be light," I quipped in nervous relief.

Msgr. Keegan looked at me with his familiar blank stare, but then gave a slight smile and said, "Truer words were never spoken, Doctor."

We continued to walk. To the right of us sat an old gray metal desk with a stack of paper neatly placed in the middle. I looked toward the other side of the room to see a few mops, a couple of industrial sized buckets, brooms, and cleaning products, all very neatly placed in the corner. The area was immaculate.

"Well, there's nothing here. We should probably go now," Msgr. Keegan uttered as we stood in the middle of the room.

Oh, no, I thought. *There's more to this story. There's something here, all right. We're not leaving just yet.*

"Monsignor, you're probably right," I said. "But let's just see what's over there." I pointed toward a darkened area that seemed to hide itself in shadow. The Monsignor complied as we continued to walk in as the isolating and eerie quiet grew. Just then, the sound of fluttering wings could be heard as a cockroach that was the size of a small mouse flew over our heads. I waved and fanned at the frightful nuisance as I let out a slight squeal.

"Oh it's just a bug, Doctor, just a bug," Msgr. Keegan added as he stood in defiance of the insect—that is, until it came in for another landing, this time on the Monsignor's head. There was no stifling his squeal: *"Hey! Get off of me!"*

We both waved and fanned at the brown roach, ultimately killing it. We looked at each other in irritated relief. "Just a bug," I mumbled.

"Did you say something, Doctor?"

"Nope," I replied as we continued to walk. "What's that?" I suddenly asked, pointing toward a neatly configured group of boxes.

"They appear to be boxes, Doctor."

"Not the boxes, Monsignor. What's that behind the boxes?" I moved one of them to reveal what seemed to be a small door about half the size of a normal one.

"This I am unaware of, Doctor." Ignoring his comment, I reached for the doorknob and of course, it was locked. I looked back at the Monsignor.

"Don't look at me," he said, shrugging his shoulders. "I don't have a key. I've never seen this door before."

"Well, Monsignor, I don't do this often. In fact, I haven't done this since I was a kid," I said as I rummaged through my purse.

"What are you looking for?"

"Ah, there it is." I retrieved a bobby pin from my purse and put it into the keyhole of the mysterious door. "I learned this from playing cops and robbers."

"I gather you played the robber."

"Good one, Monsignor," I replied jokingly as I remained focused on unlocking the door. "If memory serves me correct, all it takes is a little shove, a twist and a turn."

Click, clack went the lock as I turned the knob and pushed the door open to more darkness. "We need a light," I said. "Wait a minute." I reached into my purse for my phone and turned on its flashlight app. Msgr. Keegan nodded his head in reserved approval this time. I hunched over and stepped into the foreboding dark hole of a room. The Monsignor followed me.

The room was about the size of one of the confessionals. It was small and neat.

"What are those?" the Monsignor asked in a whisper as he pointed at dozens of pieces of paper tacked onto the walls. I moved in closer and shined the light on the biggest piece. It read: *'**James 1:15**—Then when lust hath conceived, it bringeth forth sin: and sin, when it is finished, bringeth forth death.*

"Seems like somebody's a little preoccupied with sin and death," I said as I illuminated another paper. "Look at this one." I read, *'**Romans 5:12**—Therefore, just as sin entered the world through one man, and* *death through sin, and in this way death came to all people, because all sinned.'*

I turned toward Monsignor Keegan. He stepped back and began feverishly looking around the room. "We should leave," he insisted.

"I understand, and if that's what you need to do, by all means do so. But I'm not leaving now. Not yet."

He fixed his eyes on mine and took a deep breath. "Very well, Doctor. What else do you need to see?"

I was relieved. I wasn't certain if I would have actually stayed without him, and I was glad I didn't have to find that out. I was afraid, too, but I wanted the bad guy more than I was afraid. I continued to shine the light around the paltry room.

"Just as I thought," I uttered.

"What are you talking about, Doctor?"

"I'm talking about the stool sitting there against that wall. I think someone's been listening to the confessions from in here."

"That's preposterous. Those confessionals and this church were built in 1850 with the finest of materials, with no such skullduggery in mind. I reject that notion."

"Sit here," I suggested to Monsignor Keegan, motioning toward the stool. "Do you have a phone?"

"Yes."

"Turn it on and use it for light." He did so as I walked out of the room and the custodial area. I then sat in the confessional and said, " 'Forgive me, Father, for I have sinned.' You can hear me, can't you, Monsignor?"

"Yes, I can," he replied, as I could hear him as well. I then made my way back to that hole of a room.

"Do you believe me now?" I asked him.

"Holy Mother of God," the Monsignor said in disappointed shock. "What has been going on here?"

"I think we're about to find out." I aimed the light from my phone toward an old, beat-up gray gym bag sitting next to the stool. I reached into my purse and pulled out an ink pen and the piece of cloth I use to clean my eyeglasses.

"What are you doing, Doctor?" he asked.

"Just wait." I carefully wrapped the small cloth around the zipper of the gym bag and haltingly unzipped it. I shined the now slowly dimming light from my cell phone into the bag. There they were, sure enough, a plastic bag with three blood-stained wedding bands, a covered sterling silver kukri knife, duct tape, a bottle of chloroform, and rope. The only thing missing was the gun. As I continued to move things around with the ink pen, a silver chalice that looked just like the one Monsignor Keegan had just shown me was revealed at the bottom of the bag. We looked at each other in uncomfortable confirmation with what we had just found.

"Monsig...nor, Dr. Win...ters, you sh...shouldn't be in here," said a deep, eerily melodic stuttering male voice from the other side of the door. A wave of cold fear swept through my body as the Monsignor and I looked at each other. In that moment I could see the reflection of my fears in his eyes as my phone went dead. "I kn...know you're in there," the voice continued. "I've been watching the two of you for some time now. This room is not for you. You don't have permission to be in here."

The door squeaked ajar, and a light began to shine through the entryway. One foot stepped into the room, followed by a man holding a lantern in one hand and a gun in the other. It was Church Custodian Cameron Grimes.

I glanced at Msgr. Keegan. His face was void of expression and color. I tightened my lips and gave him a reassuring nod, to no avail though. He remained petrified. As I attempted to figure this one out, the reality of this moment in time began to consume my body with immobilizing fear. I didn't know what to do. I had to admit I was not in control. Our presence in the inner sanctum of a serial killer rendered me helpless. I inhaled deeply. *This one is yours, God. I don't know what to do here. I surrender. Please take over,* I prayed to myself and exhaled. Just then, a wave of calm spilled over my body, and the paralyzing heaviness lifted.

"Mr. Grimes, right?" I asked the figure, who looked at me with a mendacious smile. "Can I call you Cameron?" He cautiously nodded in the affirmative. "And please, call me Morgan. So Cameron, I need to talk off my shoes. My feet are killing me. Okay?" He just looked at me as I removed my shoes.

"Morgan, huh? I don't care about your feet, Dr.—" he said as he looked at his wall of scriptures. "Wh...where are ma...my manners? Let me show you ahhh..round." He stuttered in painfully pulled together words as he then broke into fallacious laughter. "That's...right. I have t...to remind myself. You've al...ready ma...made your...self at home. Haaaven't you? You've even gone through ma...my belongings. Haven't you Dr. Winnnn...ters? Oh, that's right. We're friends now, huh? Ma...Morgan."

"Yes, I did, Cameron. And you have my apologies for that. I had no idea this was for you. Had I known, I certainly—Who am I kidding, Cameron? Truth be told, I found all of this stuff fascinating. The scriptures, the bag. I just wanted to know more. And Monsignor Keegan here just happened to see me looking around, and he came along."

"Re...reeally?" Cameron asked with an apparent tone of sincerity, and then squinted his eyes as he suspiciously looked at the Monsignor.

"Yes, really. Tell me about those scriptures Cameron." I went on to ask him.

I pointed to the wall lined with biblical passages. Mr. Grimes looked back and forth at Monsignor Keegan and myself. His face softened. He seemed pathetically excited that I was interested in the wall of scriptures. "That's my favorite one," I said, pointing to the biggest, *'James 1:15—Then, after desire has conceived, it gives birth to sin; and sin, when it is full-grown, gives birth to death.*

"Really? Why? Is it because it's so blunt? You know what I mean?"

"Yes there's no guessing. When sin is finished, it brings death. Right?" the hunched-over custodian said as he suddenly stood up straight, turned away from the wall, and began to speak, with no impediment. Then he raised his left hand, looked up, and began to boldly soliloquize the doctrine: *"Then, after desire has conceived, it gives birth to sin; and sin, when it is full-grown, gives birth to death.!"* He quoted in perfect diction as he looked at me. His eyes lit up as his smile grew wider. "Death, Morgan. When lust has conceived, it bringeth forth death. You hear those words? Such power, such meaning."

"Yeah," I pensively said, nodding my head in affirmation as we sat there in silence for what seemed like an eternity. Then I said, "Cameron, I'm not a biblical scholar, but I do read the Bible, and I can't remember ever having come across that one. When was the first time you heard that scripture?"

The wiry custodian started to pace back and forth in front of the door. His demeanor began to change. He was no longer standing tall. He was once again hunched over. His face became saddened. He put an old wooden chair that was off to the side in front of the door and sat in it.

"D...don't you t..try to shrink me, *Doc....tor* Win...ters!" he exclaimed as he began to stutter again. "Oh, yeah. That's right. I keep f...forgetting we're fr...friends now, *Morgan.* I...I know how this works. You're not g...getting into my head. *I* ask the questions here. Y...*You hear me? I ask the qu...questions!*" His raving rant brought about erect posture. He stood tall and almost fearless, but his stuttering reappeared in his speech with a vengeance.

"Absolutely, Cameron, absolutely. I just found that scripture to be so..."

"So wha...*what,* Doc...tor? Soooo *what?*"

"So full of life, even though it speaks to death."

He glared at me with the furrowed brow of confusion. "Well, I...I have a qu...question for you—'Morgan'." I returned his gaze with cloaked trepidation, curiosity, and feigned confidence. "What is sin?" he asked.

"Hmmm. What *is* sin?" I replied, taking a deep, contemplative breath, searching for the correct answer. "Consciously disobeying God's law," I slowly answered, resisting the temptation to ask him the same question.

Cameron then turned toward Msgr. Keegan. "Wha...what about *you*, Monsig...nor?"

"Wha—what is sin?" the clergyman asked as a lone drop of perspiration trickled down the right side of his forehead.

"Yes. What is sin? You know what? N...never mind. *Never mind!* I..I...I don't want to talk to you. You're in the business of f...forgiving sin. I wa...watched and li...listened to per...person after per...person con...fessing their sins to you. And what did you do? F...forgive 'em all. Say ten Hail Marys' and five Acts of Con...tri...tion and all's gonna be right wi..with the world. You're not doing God's work." Grimes pointed to the big scripture in the middle of the wall again. *"I'm* doing God's work. *I'm* d..d..doing God's work. Dr. Winters, if sin is the conscious disobedience of God's law, and God's law says that when sin is finished it brings death, people have to die. Right? I learned that a long time ago. A *l...long* time ago."

Grimes scratched the side of his face with his gun. His shoulders drooped again, and his face became long and full of sadness as he reflected. His guard was down. I slowly walked over and put my hand on his shoulder.

"Tell me about what you learned a long time ago, Cameron," I said softly. The silence was palpable as he looked at my hand on his shoulder and then looked me in the eye.

"Carmella t...taught me that sin...ners need to die," he said. "She taught me that."

"Who's Carmella?"

"Carmella Angela Grimes was m...my mother, tall and thin with pitch-black hair."

Like you, I thought, observing Mr. Grimes' frame.

"She slept w...with a d...different man almost e...very night, while Dad...dy worked on the rig," he continued. "One d...day when I was thir...teen, daddy went to work, and he just didn't c...come home. I never knew why he left me. I don't know wh...why he left me." The hurt and longing lay all over his face. The caretaker softened even more as he allowed his sadness to surface. "When Carmella's men would l...leave, she'd call me. *'Cameron! G...get in here and c...cclean this mess!'* she'd say."

"What was the mess, Cameron?" I softly asked, noticing he had continued to relax his posture. His legs were now open. He had rested his hands on his thighs, but still held onto the gun.

"The b...bedroom," he answered. "I st...still remember the smell."

"That must have been hard."

"No," He defensively replied. "It wa...wasn't hard, maybe. I d...don't know. I did what I had to do. I f...finally got it right. I'd cl...clean and cl...clean and cl...clean until I got it right. Otherwise, she would slap me f...four times in the face if I left anything out of place. Always f...four times. I f...finally got it right, though. I know how to take care of myself, the other sinners too, now."

"It sounds like you did, Cameron. It sounds like you did. How else did you take care of yourself?"

"When she was w...with those men, my uncles, as she w...would call them, I'd go to my room and r...read about Carmella."

"Where would you read about her? In the Bible?"

He looked at me, and then at the wall of scriptures. "Mother was a sinner," he said. "And eventually I figured out what I had to do. You know what I had to do, don't you?" He lowered his voice and began to fiendishly smile.

"You brought death to her," I replied.

"Finally, Morgan, we're on the same page." Cameron's smile widened into a toothy grin. He then began to laugh. His pained eyes went cold and vacuous. "I brought death to them all."

"Death to all of whom?"

"*The sinners!* Come on, Ma...Morgan!" he yelled as he scratched the bottom of his chin with the barrel of his gun. "The cheaters, the sanctified sluts and whores, Mrs. Victoria Gaines and Mrs. Paige Brooke and Mr. Tate. They were all married, you know, just like mother. I took care of all of them." His grammar was perfect again.

"How'd you take care of them?"

"You really want to know what am I thinking, Morgan?" Cameron asked in a more guarded, angry tone. "Of course you do, right, Doctor?"

"I only want to know what you want to tell me, Cameron," I replied as he stared at me, grasping to believe that I cared, not that I just wanted to know.

"I sat right about where you're sitting, Doctor, and heard each and every one of them confess to cheating and lying to their husbands and wives, just like Mother did. And, just like mother, they all had to die."

"What'd you do?"

"I followed them home one by one after their sinful confessions and christened them with this chalice." He reached into the black gym bag and pulled out, what looked like Msgr. Keegan's chalice. Except that it was missing few stones. This is yours Monsignor." The caretaker said looking at Msgr. Keegan. You have a replica in the sacristy." Again the caretaker flashed a bloodcurdlingly wicked grin.

"And then what?" I went on to ask.

"And then I duct-taped chloroform to their mouths and tied their hands and feet."

"Then what, Cameron?"

"I took them out to the park and made the world a better place Morgan. I killed them. I shot them four times, just like mother slapped me, and I stabbed 'em once for each year of my life that I was with my daddy before he left. I took their wedding bands out of respect for the institution they disrespected, and I left a stone from the chalice. Then I cleaned up the mess, just like I always did." His voice quivered as he caressed the handle of his gun. It was as if he became someone else when he recanted what happened.

"I think you were so strong to be able to handle all of that," I told him compassionately. "You were just a little boy. What your mother asked you to do was unconscionable. Your father left you. Little Cameron must have felt so alone. He must have felt so alone. Who was there for Cameron?"

I patiently waited for an answer as the quiet of the old church grew noisy and uncomfortable. Cameron solemnly stared off into a distance. He didn't answer.

"You must have felt so alone. Didn't you?" I paused again. "Well, you're not alone anymore, Cameron. You don't have to clean up anybody else's mess anymore. You're not alone anymore. You don't have to do any of this anymore. You're not alone."

I pulled the stool next to Mr. Grimes and sat down on it. Then I gently put my arm around his shoulder and pressed his head against my bosom. "You're not alone anymore, Cameron. You're not alone anymore."

He dropped his weapon to the floor and began to sob in my arms. I held Mr. Grimes while signaling Msgr. Keegan with my eyes to pick up the gun. He did.

Just then, a faint voice calling my name could be heard from the nave of the church. "Wintahs? You in here, Wintahs?" Relief permeated my entire being as Slade's voice rang clear. "Wintahs?"

"We're in here, Commander. In here," Msgr. Keegan excitedly shouted back as he held onto Mr. Grimes's gun and I continued to cradle the emotionally regressed caretaker.

"Where?"

"Behind the confessional."

Slade began to enter as he hunched over to fit into the doorway of the small room. "What the hell?" he whispered as he took in the visual of myself holding a crying Mr. Grimes, a wall full of pieces of paper with scriptures written on them, and, last but certainly not least, Monsignor Keegan awkwardly standing in the middle of the tiny room holding a gun.

"Here, Commander. Take this," the Monsignor said as he nervously handed the gun to Slade.

∽ CHAPTER 20 ∾

Once again, the dark of night was interrupted by flashing lights and police radios as Cameron Grimes was escorted in handcuffs by two police officers out of the front door of the old Sacred Heart Cathedral.

"He's gotta go on suicide watch, Slade," I said to my comrade as we stood outside the church, myself wrapped in one of those gray blankets, watching Mr. Grimes be put into a squad car. Msgr. Keegan, also draped in a blanket as well, was a few feet away, talking with a couple of other clergymen who had arrived on the scene.

"Yeah, I told 'em," Slade replied as I took a sip of water from a bottle that had been given to me.

"Slade, I tell you, it never ceases to amaze me how the very same coping mechanisms that can help a child survive horrendous neglect, abandonment and abuse can talk that same emotionally stunted adult man-child into murdering someone," I said. "Ya know what I mean?"

"Yeah, I know, Wintahs," Slade compassionately responded to my own momentary attempt to cope with what had just taken place.

"After all these years of practicing psychiatry, all the people I've seen and tried to help, I'm still at a loss when it comes to helping people who need help and won't get it," I said. "Instead, they take matters into their own hands, and blame it on God's law, while still just trying to avoid pain. For him it was pain delayed in order to survive as a child. But there's no escaping that pain, Slade. Sooner or later, one way or another it catches up with you. Truth be told, how many adults roam around, not dealing with past hurts. But instead of killing people, they're drinking or drugging, or spending or manipulating. You name it, Slade, and people are doing it instead of feeling it."

"Excuse me, Commander, Dr. Winters, but we need to get a few more statements from you," said a police officer who had walked up to us.

"Okay, here I come," I responded.

"Want some company?" Slade asked as I looked into his warm brown eyes and then smiled.

"Thanks, but I got this one. I know the drill." Slade and I tapped water bottles in a toast of accord as I walked away with the officer.

*   *   *   *

It had been about three weeks since Cameron Grimes had been taken into custody. It was ten o'clock

Monday morning, and I was putting lipstick on in the ladies' room of New Orleans' Morial Convention Center, where I had been asked to be the keynote speaker at the Greater New Orleans Adults for Boys and Girls Foundation year-end event. Out of all the nonprofit organizations in New Orleans, this had become the most widely recognized and well-attended event of its type in the region. Over forty thousand people were expected to be in attendance. I stood there, holding the twenty-minute-long speech in my hand as I gazed into the mirror.

"Boys, girls, men, women. You should be proud of yourselves," I tried to confidently say out loud, but then I cringed at the thought of going on with the speech. *It is what it is, Morgan,* I thought as I grabbed a piece of tissue and began to blot my lipstick. It's a good speech, but it wasn't from my heart. It was from my head. My heart was telling me that I needed to talk about my journey over the last few weeks. And my cautious, protective, and dependable head wanted me to stick to the script.

I heard a knock on the door. "You're up, Dr. Winters," said a voice on the other side. I walked out of the bathroom and into the main hall just in time to hear myself introduced. There were people almost as far as the eye could see.

"Most of you know about our keynote speaker, Dr. Morgan Winters," boomed the emcee. "She was born and reared right here in New Orleans, Louisiana, and she is a *magna cum laude* graduate from our own Tulane University. After receiving two bachelor's degrees—one in psychology, and the other one in biology—she went onto Yale, where she received her degree in medicine. Then she completed her residency in psychiatry at Columbia University. New York had her up there for seven years, where she did a fellowship and became the attending psych doctor at Harlem Hospital. After those seven years, the good doctor decided she'd been away from home long enough, and, thank God for us, she came home."

Spontaneous applause erupted as I looked out at the audience from behind the curtain. I spotted Slade and Kendall a few rows back.

"She's been featured in countless magazine articles and journals, reaching out to so many with her insights on the workings of the human mind. She's been on the covers of *Psycho-Socio Today, American Mind, New York Journal of Psychiatry, US World, People Today, New Orleans Weekly* magazines. And we hold her in particularly high esteem for the wonderful work she's done and continues to do with the New Orleans police department."

More plaudits filled the room. Just then, I was able to make eye contact with Slade for a reassuring smile and wink of the eye.

"Without further ado, ladies and gentlemen, please welcome *Dr. Morgan Jane Winters!*" Thunderous applause erupted as I walked onto the stage.

"Thank you so much. Thank you. Thank you," I said as the accolades continued and I gazed out into the sea of people. I patiently waited for the room to quiet before starting to speak. "Thank you so much. That's very humbling," I said in a *sotto voice.* Suddenly, my hands grew cold, and my heart began to race at the thought of giving the speech I had written. Somehow it didn't feel right. I paused for a moment. *Come on, Morgan. That voice is telling you something. Listen to it,* I thought.

And then it hit me. Even though this was the speech, that my mind, my intellect, that *I* had decided to write and give, this wasn't the speech God had in mind for me. *It's time to talk about what you've been through Morgan, not just what you know. I surrender.* I thought. I looked up at the many faces looking back at me and summarily began to tear the speech up. The crowd instinctively erupted in supportive applause.

"I surrender!" I firmly stated into the microphone. "Say it with me! *I surrender!*"

Jill Collins was reared in the historical Pontchartrain Park subdivision of New Orleans, LA where she grew up singing and playing her flute in the church choir. She earned a Bachelor of Arts in Sociology from Tulane University while working as a full-time Researcher. She would then go on to work as a full time Research Associate at Louisiana State University (LSU) for over thirteen years. She now resides in Silver Spring, MD with her husband.

Jill's first outing, 'Surrender' is the first in a series of novels centered around fictional character, psychiatrist and part-time sleuth Morgan Jane Winters. The series has been warmly dubbed as 'Murder Mysteries With a Message'. Be sure to check out her next novel, 'Hide and Seek', coming soon.

To know more about Jill visit her web page:

www.Jillcollins.net